Someone to Hold Me
The Gods Made Me Do It #6
By Lisa Oliver

Someone to Hold Me (The Gods Made Me Do It #6)

Someone To Hold Me is a work of fiction. Names, characters, places and incidents are either the product of the author's imagination or are used fictitiously and any resemblance to any actual persons, living or dead, events or locales is entirely coincidental.

Table of Contents

Dedication

My heart goes out to those victims of hate crimes and anyone who feels as though they are "different". Please know you are loved.

To my readers, you are the light in my soul.

Huge thanks to Amanda and Phil for keeping my facts straight and my prose polished. Any mistakes are all mine.

This was my 60th book – woo hoo.

Quick Author's Note

My books are professionally edited, however sometimes mistakes are missed, and the responsibility for that is all mine. When I was writing this story, I was having an issue with apostrophes, in particular, those relating to possession. In books I've written in the past, I have always used the "s's" system – like in Nereus's story, where I didn't have a problem using the extra "s". However, for some reason in Hades' story that didn't seem right, so the lack of the extra "s" is deliberate and from what I understand about grammar, is perfectly correct provided I am consistent with it.

As for the facts in this story, I have used fictious license again, as I have with the other Gods stories. Hades is the Lord of the Underworld. Zeus and Poseidon are two of his brothers. He does have a big dog called Cerberus and he was "married" to Persephone who was known as "the dread Queen Persephone."

One issue from my editors was that I mentioned that Persephone was Hades' niece – which she was, as her mother was Demeter who was Hades' sister. While in modern times we would consider such a relationship far too close for comfort, scholars tell us the Olympians had no such concerns. I haven't shied away from the family connection, but hopefully you will like what I've done.

If you have any questions, please don't hesitate to contact me using the details at the back of the story. As with all my stories, my aim is to make you smile.

Lisa ☺

Chapter One

"Twice in one month, brother. Some little cutie must have caught your eye. How come you're lurking back here, instead of pumping your cock into the delightful cuties' ass in one of the back rooms."

"Not everything's about sex, Sei, as you should know by now." Hades didn't bother turning around. His brother would seem as though he was talking to the pole Hades was leaning on and that was fine by him. If he wanted to be seen by the others in Claude's club then he would have shown himself.

"Aww, are you having some problems in the dick department," Poseidon teased. "Maybe you need something special to get your equipment working again. Tell me what you need, and I'll point you in the right direction. We cater for all types here."

"The only one being a problem dick around here is you. There's never been anything wrong with my equipment," Hades said, stung more than he probably should be. "Can't a guy just lurk once in a while?"

"Hey, yeah, you know you're always welcome here." Poseidon's shoulder nudged at Hades' arm as he leaned on the same pole. "We've got amazing scenery here; you have to admit that. There must be someone here who catches your eye."

"So many handsome faces, but there's no light," Hades said sadly, looking over the crowd of healthy shifters dancing, laughing and so much more. "I keep looking for the light, that spark that tells me my forever's finally in my sight, but I can't find it."

"You've been talking to Lasse again." Sei shook his head. "I know my sons, Sebastian, hell, even that dickhead Thor keeps talking about those mystical lights when they found their mates, but I didn't see one when I met Claude."

"Are you sure about that?" Hades looked down at his younger brother. In human form, he was at least a foot taller than the God of the Sea. "Hells teeth, you were probably that blinded by lust you couldn't see past Claude's magnificent abs and huge package."

"Meh. Maybe." Hades noticed Sei didn't deny his description. "I felt a pull, and I will admit to not caring what Claude was to me so long as he used that cock of his to my advantage."

"And now you're in love, raising twins and so domesticated it would've made your teeth ache in another life." Hades went back to perusing the crowds. "I want that for me, well, the love side of things. You can keep the twins."

"You keep coming back here. Are you sure...?"

"I come back here because it's one of the few places I can get laid without everyone shuddering for all the wrong reasons the moment I come into view. I come here because for a few short hours I can be seen as a man, instead of some mystical horror story whose name should never be mentioned. Your pack coped with a

Kraken landing in the middle of the club. They barely shiver at me."

"Yeah, fun times." Sei grinned, and then his grin got wider as he spotted his mate coming down the stairs. Hades lifted a hand in a wave, well aware Claude was as immune to his invisibility as his brother was, but Claude was clearly astute enough to stay at the bar, rather than coming over to see him.

"You know," Sei said thoughtfully, rubbing his chin. "Maybe you're looking for the wrong type, in the wrong place."

"Do not suggest any more of your ridiculous places," Hades said quickly. "It was bad enough the last time. Thanks to you, I've tried human clubs. I went to a dozen libraries. I wandered around a supermarket and tried sitting on park benches. I even, Fates forbid, went to a human gym." He shuddered. "Do you know how ridiculous I look in shorts? It didn't make any difference. No one would come near me in any of those places. You know my curse better than any man. The whole not speaking my name concept must be genetically ingrained in the entire human race by now, even if they're not aware of it."

"Your mate's not likely to be human," Sei said. "I might not think much of the old biddies who join our threads with others, but even they wouldn't be that cruel."

Hades wasn't so sure. "I'm feeling my age, Sei. All I have to look forward to at home is the incessant noise of Cerberus's howling."

"You still haven't let him out then?" Sei smirked.

"After what he did to Lasse?" Hades shook his head. "He's lucky he's just chained up and not rotting in Tartarus. The Hellhounds do a good job of guarding the gates. No one can get past them. I just don't know where else to look. I've hiked trails in a dozen countries, I've camped. In a tent. My gods, have you any idea how basic that is? I had to pee in the bloody bushes. I've gone to auctions in London, New York, and Paris. I've spent enough time lurking around

Lasse and Jason's place in Greece to have their little one calling me uncle. I've trolled the streets of Las Vegas, now that was fun. Weird is acceptable there, but it didn't make any difference. I've visited a dozen packs, invisibly of course, but I still haven't seen that elusive damn light."

"But who are you looking at?" Sei prodded gently. Hades gave a mental vote of thanks to the Fates for his brother's mating. A year before Hades never imagined having such a conversation. "When you look out at the scene here, who do you see?"

"I see cute little wolves looking for strong mates. Blonds, dark haired, even that little red head with the freckles. So damn cute, every one of them, but none of them are my mate."

"None of the Doms tickle your fancy?"

"I don't want to fight for my fuck on a daily basis," Hades snapped. "Thor might be into that sort of thing but not me."

"And Thor is mated to the cutest little cat shifter you've ever seen – a man who adores books."

Hades felt a shiver run down his spine at the thought of Orin's special book – it held the only spell in existence that could summon a living ancient god. Sei had teased him a dozen times about the loving pair inviting him for dinner, through the use of the spell. Hades sent a large gift basket when he heard about the arrival of their children with a short note explaining he was traveling and would visit on his return.

"You see," Sei said, stretching away from the pole. "I think those Fates know more than they let on, but don't you dare mention I said so," he added quickly. "But," he went on, "if you think about the mates we've all snagged so far, not one of them was what we expected, but every one of them was what we needed."

"Are you boring your kids to sleep with psychology books again?"

"Only sometimes, but then my kids are geniuses, so it's expected."

Sei waited as if he expected Hades to agree, but Hades just smirked and waited.

"Fine," Sei huffed. "The thing is, despite the number of shifters who'd graciously taken us on, not everyone got a wolf for a start. Thor has a cat. Lasse snagged a sphinx for goodness sake. That set Artie's hair on fire just thinking about it. And Artie – another classic example. He didn't get a shifter or a twink and he expected both. I did wonder if the Fates had got their braids twisted or something, because Thor's mate would be far more suited to Artie in my opinion, but then despite the odds, all of them are deliriously happy."

Hades' frown deepened. "The Fates would never pair me with another god, not from any pantheon. No god could handle living in the Underworld."

"You don't live there all the time," Sei pointed out. "I have to go. My mate is getting restless...."

"You're horny because you've been watching that threesome in the corner for the past five minutes." It was a good scene, but Hades' cock barely reacted. Sei on the other hand was bristling with arousal.

"Fine, I'm going to find my mate and see if he'll wrap his juicy lips around my cock. Happy? As for you, bro, maybe you need to shed the mantle of gloom you carry and stop thinking about your position as a curse. And get out more," he yelled as he walked away. "If your mate's not where you've been then you need to go somewhere else."

Go somewhere else. Hades' lips tightened as the ache in his gut increased. Closer to Sei than their brother Zeus, Hades knew his brother was trying to be supportive. But watching as Sei was readily embraced by his huge smiling mate, Hades' sense of loneliness threatened to overwhelm him. Taking one last look at the redhead with adorable freckles, Hades disappeared back to his domain. It was time to gag that damn dog of his so he could get some sleep.

/~/~/~/~/

"Hades?" The orb rattled on Hades' desk. "Hades, are you there? Answer me." The orb rattled again. "Damn it, Hades."

"What do you want now, brother of mine?" Hades asked through gritted teeth. It'd been three weeks since his last visit to Sei and Claude's club. Since that time, he'd written, read, got caught up on his records, and refused to do anything for Cerberus except give him a mute button. Souls were pouring in faster than he could process them, and instead of how things were back in the good old days where all souls came to the Underworld for processing, thanks to the advent of a variety of gods, Hades got stuck with the truly evil ones. That meant organizing more demons, increasing the guards at the gates. Charon was threatening to go on strike because none of those who demanded passage thought to pay him anymore. *The old ways were far more efficient,* Hades thought with a sigh.

"I did it, I finally did it." Sei's orb cackled with excitement. "I asked Claude to marry me and he said yes. Can you believe it? He said yes."

"I can't imagine your mate refusing you anything," Hades said, momentarily overcome by memories of his own failed relationship with Persephone. "Haven't you been married before?"

Poseidon's scoff came through loud and clear. "I have bedded more than it would take a thousand story tellers to tell, but I always believed marriage had to be to someone special."

"And Claude is your special someone." Hades couldn't stay bitter, not when Sei's orb was shining so brightly in his dim domain. "I am truly happy for you, brother, although I shudder at the thought of what a mortal clergyman might make of you and Claude."

"There'll be no clergy at our wedding," Sei's laughter rang around the hollow walls of Hades' office. "Shawn, the shifter guardian from the Cloverleah pack has agreed to marry us, or bind us, according to wolf shifter ritual."

"Er… don't wolves have some archaic custom where if they are going through the bonding ritual with a non-wolf, that other wolves can challenge them for the right to mate?"

"Yes! Won't it be exciting, that's why I need you to come, Hades, please. I need you there."

Hades frowned. "You're wanting me to scare away any of the puppies who threaten your mate and mating?"

"Hell no." Poseidon's laughter made his orb dance around the desk. Hades reached for it, before it shattered on the floor. "Claude is relishing a fight. One of the shifters, Griff from the Cloverleah pack was in the other night, crowing about how he had to fight sixty challenges to mate with his cat shifter Diablo. Claude is hoping to best that record."

"So, you want me to fight wolves on your behalf?"

"Meh. It might come to that, I won't know until the day, but no, I want you here, supporting me, and...."

"Yes?"

"I'm not allowed to interfere with any of the challenge fights." Hades imagined Sei's pouty face and bit his lip to stop himself from laughing out loud. "It's sounds dreary, but my hunky mate tells me that I'm not allowed to use my powers and wash away the challengers. I'm also not allowed to call my Kraken, mermen, or set off large cracks in the challenge circle. Honestly, these wolves have so many rules."

"So, the plan is for me to do those things, or stop you doing them?" As the eldest brother, only Hades had the power to stop Poseidon or Zeus from doing anything.

"You're supposed to stop me, at least that's what I told Claude you'd do, but...."

"If Claude is agreeable to my being there, then I will do as he requested," Hades said firmly, knowing immediately what Poseidon was going to ask. "I can sit on you while the challenges are going on and then leave when the festivities start."

"NO! Hades, you have to stay. Zeus won't bother to show up, he's being rude and arrogant about my marrying a wolf shifter. Personally, I think he's just jealous because no one can put up with his fat ass for longer than five minutes. But there will be representatives from every other pantheon in existence there for the binding ceremony as well as countless wolves from packs all over the country – apparently this is a big deal. You could find that shining light you're looking for."

"Or, I could scare everyone away and no one will have a good time at all." The anxiety in Hades' gut churned just thinking about all those people in one place.

"I want you there, Hades, please." Oh, it was no wonder Poseidon could calm the waters. When he put on his persuasive voice, Hades was powerless to resist. "Stand by my side. Stop me doing something stupid. I want this so much. I've had the rings for months. I finally got up the courage to ask him and I don't want to fuck it up now."

And if anyone could fuck things up, it's Sei. His mouth alone is legendary. "You know I'll come. Let me know when and where and Sei, I'm truly proud of you for doing this. After countless millennia of not binding yourself to anyone... I'm glad Claude is the one for you."

"I want this. I know marriage is more of a merger or power thing among our kind, but the humans had the right idea about it. I finally know what it's like to have a family," Sei said quietly. "It's not just the twins, my other sons will be there too with their mates, and Baby of course. Artie said he'd had a bit of trouble, but they've both promised to come to the wedding. But I need you when I stand before all others and make my commitment to my mate. Only you know the full extent of what we've been through. We share a wealth of history you and I."

Ancient history. There were times Hades forgot where he came from, or how he ended up where he was. Time softened all memories, but he knew what Poseidon was talking about. "I'll be there, by your side. You have my word."

In typical Poseidon fashion, the orb disappeared without any goodbyes, but Hades knew he'd been heard. *Weddings, weddings. What do I know about...?* Sweeping a hand across his desk, Hades consigned all his papers to a heap on the side. "Folsom get your ass in here," he yelled.

"My lord, yes my Lord." His PA, Folsom stumbled in, tripping over a non-existent step in the doorway.

Hades raised an eyebrow at his PA's appearance. "I'm not sure purple and burnt orange are a good color combination on you," he said, eyeing the bright tie dyed shirt, and huge purple pants that were hanging precariously low on Folsom's hips.

Folsom's dark green skin and hair clashed terribly with his clothes.

"I made them myself." Folsom picked himself up off the floor. "It's not easy keeping up with the latest fashions when I'm not allowed to go topside. Amazon won't deliver and any of the television programs we get down here are years out of date. If I could just...."

"No," Hades said firmly. "I still remember what happened last time you were allowed to go topside. You burnt down an entire shopping block. The papers said it was a gas leak, but I know it was you."

"They didn't have the shirt I wanted in my size, and they said it would take two weeks to order one in," Folsom stamped his foot and a spurt of flame licked the sole of his boot. "I knew you wouldn't let me go up again so soon, and I didn't have an address to get the thing sent to me...."

"We have a communal post box set up in every capital city in the world. You can get things delivered. Stop your pouting. You're not going. Now,

I want you to research wedding gifts. For the man who has everything. I want something extra special."

"It would be easier to shop if I could...."

"I want the gift to come from this world. We have many treasures here. I want one selected and gift wrapped properly."

"Gift wrapped." Folsom gulped. "And who's names should I put on the card? I'll need an address too."

"Poseidon and his mate Claude are getting married. I will be attending the wedding, so I'll take the gift myself." Hades got up from his desk, ignoring Folsom's incredulous look. "Have it done by the end of the day and get rid of those papers on my desk."

"All of them?" Folsom eyed the pile with a wary glance.

"All of them. I'm sick to death of paperwork. I'm going to inspect the guards at the gate and speak to Charon. I'll be out for the rest of the day."

"Lady Persephone wants to talk to you and…"

"I'm going out."

Hades knew the final note in his tone would have Folsom agreeing to his orders, although he had no doubt half of the papers at least would reappear in the next day's pile. But for now, he wanted to be alone. There were a host of souls waiting for him to set up torture routines, and there'd been three messages from Persephone he assumed he had to answer at some stage. But if Charon was unhappy in his job, then Hades had to deal with that first, and then feed the whining Cerberus and maybe… just maybe…. Hades sighed. It was the maybe that was killing him inside. There was no one to have any maybes with.

Chapter Two

Red dinner jacket with black pants? *Too pretentious.* Maybe jeans? *Too casual for a wedding.* What about the gray suit? *Can't fight wolves in that.* Hades turned up the corner of his lip at his clothing choices. Worrying about what to wear to his brother's wedding was stupid, but he couldn't help himself. For three weeks he'd worried, fretted, reaching for an orb to cancel a dozen times since he'd got the call. But now the time had arrived, and all Hades had to show for it was a disorganized wardrobe, bare skin, a knot in his stomach the size of a melon and a sickly taste in his mouth.

Looking at the mess in his closet, Hades held out a hand, causing an orb to appear. *It'd be so easy. Sei will be flat out busy. Just leave him a message, citing an emergency and you can get on with your day.* But it was the 'getting on with your day' that was the problem. There was nothing in Hades' day except more of the same – more people to draft up torture routines for, more paperwork to sign, more complaints to listen to and more of Cerberus's whining.

My mate isn't going to find me down here, and while Hades thought his chances of finding the light he was looking for at Sei's wedding was remote at best, *I'd be networking, I'd be doing something I don't usually do and that's what Sei said I should be doing.* Heaving a sigh, Hades tossed the orb on the bed, dropped the towel hanging loosely around his hips and waved his arms. *There. Dressed. Basic black. It's what I'm known for anyway.* The leather pants clung to his legs like a second skin, the button up shirt was tight across his chest.

Grabbing his long leather coat from the hook on the door of the closet, Hades slid into it, barely noticing the weight on his shoulders. The coat was crafted from the finest leather, woven with spells, and fitted perfectly to the upper part of his frame before it flared out from the waist. His coat of armor, Persephone called it and Hades winced at the memory. He still hadn't returned his ex's calls. *I'm busy, madam,* he thought as he scooped up the present Folsom had managed to wrap somewhat successfully. *See, I do have a social life, even if it is only thanks to my brother.*

Pushing back his negative thoughts, Hades hovered for one more minute, eying the orb on the bed. *Fuck it, can't back out now.* Closing his eyes, Hades thought of his brother and translocated out of his bedroom.

/~/~/~/~/

"Ali, you came." Aloysius Thorndyke Barrington Garcia fumbled with his bulky present, almost dropping it before Claude took it from his hands, depositing it on a handy table. "I was so pleased you agreed to come. You missed the challenges."

"I knew you'd win," Ali suppressed the shiver he got when he thought about wolves fighting, and beamed at his tall hunky friend. "Look at you, all married and bonded. Mated life must agree with you."

"It has its moments," Claude's smile was just as wide. "You haven't met my Sei, yet, have you?"

"Oh, it's Sei, is it?" Ali laughed. "Only you could claim bonds with an ancient god. For those of us a little lower on the food chain, we know to refer to them by their titles, not their nicknames. One doesn't want to be pinned down by a misplaced trident, now do we?"

"Sei will adore you," Ali found himself smothered in a hug that threatened his breath. While he had a healthy distrust for wolf shifters for the most part, Claude had always been one of the good guys. Although Ali was doubting his decision as he struggled for breath. But Claude pulled back before his face was completely beetroot red. "Come and meet him and see for yourself."

"I thought he'd be easy to pick out from the crowd. Isn't he like seven foot tall or something with green hair?" Ali followed his tall friend who plowed through the onlookers easily. There were wolves everywhere, some

Ali recognized as being pack and others who'd probably come for the challenges. An Alpha mating ritual, as Claude explained it to him, was one time when wolves came together from all kinds of packs. It was only Claude's reassurance that once the challenges were over, everyone came together as friends, that saw Ali dusting off his best duds and spending hours choosing a suitable gift for his friend's special day.

"He only looks like that when he's pissed off." Claude stopped in front of an incredible looking blond. "Babe, I'd like you to meet Aloysius Thorndyke Barrington Garcia, aka Ali. He saved my life once back in the nineteen twenties and we've stayed good friends ever since."

"You saved my mate's life?" The blond's eyes raked him up and down as if he had no clothes on.

Ali raised his chin and straightened his spine. "You're Poseidon, Lord of the Sea? You don't look tall enough. I imagined some big beefy bloke with a shiny tail and green hair. You're barely taller than I am."

Sei exchanged heated looks with his mate. "This one's got spunk. I like it."

"His spunk saved my life once," Claude agreed, his grin still firmly in place. "I was trapped in my wolf form, in a cage, by some hunters who were threatening to skin me alive. I was barely conscious – the guys had shot me, and I was bleeding bad. This little guy was sitting up a tree munching his nuts, saw what happened and came flying down, ran up inside this one hunter's trousers and bit him in the balls. Came flying out, leapt off that one guy's boots and attacked the other guy with a full on facial, claws and teeth. Up and down, round and round. He was moving so fast they couldn't see him – he was just a blur. After about two minutes they took off running screaming the devil was after them. Ali shifted, got me out of the cage and we've been friends ever since."

"That was extremely brave of you. I think you'll be one of my new friends too," Sei said warmly holding out his hand. Ali took it and shook it tentatively, a teensy bit worried the god wouldn't appreciate his sparkling personality. "So, tell me, little cutie," Sei didn't let go of his hand, "are you here with anyone? Do you have a significant other who maybe couldn't make it to our auspicious event?"

Surely, he's not hitting on me. "No," Ali tried to pull his hand away. "No, my scurry doesn't approve of my association with wolves, well, they don't approve of my association with anyone really. They're a snobby bunch. I'm quite alone, and quite capable of looking after myself, thank you very much. Er, haven't you got vows to make and things like that?" *Will you let go of my hand?*

"It is just about that time, babe." Claude stroked down his mate's long hair. "Are you sure you're ready to pledge yourself to a scruffy wolf like me?"

"After all that fighting you did for me this morning?" Sei huffed, but at least he let go of Ali's hand so he could wrap his arm around Claude's waist. "I'd be stupid to back out now. I just thought, if Ali didn't have a date for this evening, he could keep my friend company."

"Your friend?" Claude's eyes widened. "Oh, you mean…."

"Yes, I think it'd be fun, don't you?" Poseidon interrupted smoothly. Ali found himself the recipient of a charm offensive. "You don't mind, do you?" The god purred, "only my friend doesn't get out much and he has this silly idea that people shun him for no reason at all. I'm sure if he just smiled once in a while…."

"Babe, we have to get to the challenge circle. Shawn, the shifter guardian is waiting on us." Ali shook himself as Claude tapped his mate on the arm. The god of the sea certainly had a persuasive way about him, although Ali wasn't sure how much of it was natural charm.

"I'll come and watch the ceremony," Ali said quickly. "You go and do your thing. We can catch up after and you can introduce me to your *friend*."

Probably an ex-lover or something he's palming off to me, so Claude doesn't get upset. Meh, at least Sei said he'd be quiet. We'll see.

The crowds were moving through into the main hall of the club. Ali eyed the crush of people and then looked back at the huge tables groaning under the weight of the food. *Ninety percent of the people here are taller than me – I'm not going to see anything anyway.* Making his decision, Ali scuttled over to the tables and picked up a clean plate. *Oh, my gods, the wolves put on a good spread.*

Chapter Three

Hades stood on the outside of the challenge circle that still smelled of fresh paint and the blood of the wolves Claude and his friends had challenged. *Such a barbaric idea,* he thought trying not to dwell on the fact that despite the room being crammed full of men and the occasional woman, no one got too close to him.

A tall alpha wolf, not as tall as Claude but healthily sized nonetheless stood beside him, but he only had eyes for the shifter guardian waiting on the alpha pair. *Kane,* Hades remembered Sei mentioning him as the alpha of the Cloverleah pack – the tiny pack that took out the dark elves. His second Griff, who was standing on the other side of his alpha kept giving him curious glares, but Hades was well used to ignoring them.

"Everyone, if we can begin." Shawn didn't raise his voice, but then in a room dominated by shifters he didn't have to. There were a few non shifters in the room. Hades noticed Ra and his entourage across the circle from him. Their eyes met, and Ra briefly nodded before his eyes slid away. Thanatos was in the crowd, holding his wee mate up on his shoulders so the tiny shifter could see. Hades picked out Thor and Orin, his nephews Artemas, Lasse, and Nereus along with their mates. Baby was dressed more somberly than usual, but he was standing between Artemas and Silvanus which was not like him. He was holding onto Athena and Tony's hands as if they were trying to get away. Zeus was no where to be seen, of course. *Snobby sod.*

"We have come here today to witness the Alpha Mating Ritual between Claude, Alpha of the Tulsa pack and son of Fenrir, to Poseidon, Lord of the Sea." Hades stopped looking around the crowd for familiar faces and turned his attention to the middle of the circle. Poseidon and Claude both wore suits, but it was their faces that captured Hades' attention. *All they can see is each other.* Hades' heart almost stopped it ached so much.

"This is not something that is to be undertaken lightly, as this bond, like any governed by the Fates is unbreakable by any among us." Shawn smiled as he looked around the silent crowd. "It is usual at this point to ask if anyone has any objections, but as Claude and his friends bested all of the challenges placed this morning, I'm not going to. The Fates wove the threads of these two men together a long time ago. No one here will interfere."

"If anyone dares raise their voice against us, I'll call the Kraken again," Sei threatened. There were a few laughs but the men from Tulsa looked uncomfortable.

"At this point," Shawn continued smoothly, "I'd like to ask Claude to speak to those present and explain why he chose Poseidon above all others, for himself and the pack."

"Aw babe," Claude's voice was gentle and full of love as he looked at his mate. "As if there was anyone else in existence who could steal my heart like you did. You swanked in here, grabbed me by the crotch and thereby started me on a ride I never want to get off. When you left, I wept in silence, but I knew you'd come back and you did, in spectacular style – threatening my pack with that damn Kraken of yours, which we still talk about today."

The laughter was louder this time. Claude's eyes never left Sei's face as he waited for it to die down. "You are my world, Lord of the Sea. You are the reason I get up in the morning, and your taste is on my lips every night when I fall asleep. Your beautiful body has blessed me with two wondrous children and through you, my family has grown to encompass four other sons I'm proud to call my own. I don't have the words to explain the way my heart sings for you, my wolf howls for you and my loins stir only for you. You are my love, my life and my everything, standing proud by my side till the end of time – there will never be another for me."

"You are such a softy, babe." Was that a spark of tears Hades saw in Poseidon's eyes?

"And so," Claude's voice rose, "I ask all those present to accept Poseidon, Lord of the Sea, as my mate and my partner, standing equal with me on land, as I swim beside him below the waters."

Hades wanted to cover his ears as howls of approval shook the walls of the room. A peak at Ra made him want to laugh. Ra's fingers were jammed into his ears, and his eyes were scrunched tight. The two little ones, Athena and Tony didn't seem to mind the noise, tilting their heads back, their little yips joining in with the rest of them.

It was quite a few minutes before Shawn could speak again. "And now, Lord Poseidon, can you explain to those present why it is you chose Claude and why you agreed to become alpha mate of the Tulsa pack."

This will be interesting. Hades folded his hands in front of him as he waited to hear his brother speak. Poseidon was never serious, unless he was angry about something, and Hades rarely heard him say anything remotely sappy.

But Poseidon surprised him. Clicking his fingers, his trident appeared, causing more than one gasp in the crowd. Watching his mate, Sei bent, laying the trident at Claude's feet before he straightened again and took Claude's hands in his. "For you, I would give up the sea," he said quietly. "Since the beginning of time I have moved as my beloved waves, never settling, never attaching myself to anyone. Ebbing, flowing, always moving, I smashed the bonds of rock and seaweed that sought to tie me to one place. And then I met you."

"You shone," Poseidon's voice rose. "Your heart's call was more powerful than any siren. You taught me what love truly means – not the worship of a thousand voices, but the gentle murmur of the one that holds me close at night. You stood fast when I was buffeted by the winds of doubt and you never gave up on me."

"You gave me a home." Poseidon sniffed as his voice lowered again. "You gave me hope when I had none, strength when I needed it, and the urge to do better for those I consider family. Some might say it is impossible to stop the flow of the tides, but for you, I would do it in an instant. I love you and because I love you, I will take on these mangy wolves that cling to us like barnacles, keep them safe, and do my best to be the Alpha Mate you deserve. My world is at your feet," he indicated the trident. "I wouldn't do that for anybody else but you."

"Oh Sei." Claude was crying, openly, tears pouring down his wide and handsome face as the wolves howled and yelled around them. Hades was moved, and more than a little bit jealous, but as the crowd quieted, and Shawn wove some elaborate spell cementing the two men's bonds well past the afterlife, he felt a shaft of hope as well. *Surely the Fates wouldn't favor one brother more than the other.*

/~/~/~/~/

"Hey there little bushy tail, do you think you can stretch those lips of yours wide enough to take me down your delicious throat?"

Ali looked up from his plate which was sitting on his knees. All he could see was legs and hips, and yes, while the package sitting at eye level might look tempting, the words were enough to put his back up. Lifting his eyes higher, and higher and higher, *why did wolf shifters have to be so tall,* he smirked, just a little. "Not interested, thank you."

He watched as an incredulous look came over the wolf's face. And then it was as though a light bulb went off. "Oh, you're not from around these parts. You didn't know what I meant." The man slid his thumbs into his waistband framing the ever growing package and his lewd smirk got wider. "I'm offering you my dick to suck. Now, I don't want no drooling, mind you. I don't need no slobber stains on my new pants. But if you open up nice and wide, I'm sure I'll slip right in."

"You'll slip right in – your cock in my mouth, is that what you're saying?" Ali glanced to the side of the thighs, but Claude was on the other side of the room. He carefully put his half-finished plate on the floor and sat up straight. "I'm sitting here enjoying my meal. What made you think I wanted to suck your cock, when I had a mouth full of lamb stew?"

"You're a hearty eater." That look of confusion was back. "I've been watching you. You're not here with anyone else."

"That's very observant of you. But how did my eating lamb stew lead you to think I wanted to give you a blowjob?" If the wolf had half a brain, Ali might have considered it. He'd been through a long dry spell lately and he wasn't immune to the testosterone flowing around the party. But dumbasses turned his libido into the permanent off position.

"Well, of course you wanted to give me a blowjob. Everyone does. But hopefully you won't be too slobbery...."

"Because you don't want any stains on your new pants. I got that the first time." Ali shook his head. "You don't have to worry about me leaving any marks on your shiny pants, because I'm not going to suck you."

Two straight lines appeared in the furrow between the wolf's eyes. "Why not? Is there something wrong with your little brain? Look, I know you prey animals aren't that bright, but my dick is right here, and you made me horny."

"You... you...," Ali huffed as he pushed back his chair, jumping to his feet and setting his fists on his hips. "How the hell did I make you horny? I was eating my dinner."

"You're eating, chewing, swallowing. You've got sexy lips. I want them around my cock. I waited until your plate was almost empty."

"No you didn't, you selfish git. I was only half finished. But that's beside the point. Have I got 'I give blowjobs after dinner' painted on my forehead?" He tapped the spot where his third eye would be. This guy was going to give him a headache.

The man leaned down, peering at Ali's forehead. "Did you get a tattoo or something? I can't see it, but I know this guy…."

"I'm sure you know a lot of guys and half of them would probably be on their knees for you right now, but I'm not one of them." *Maybe this guy got dropped on his head at birth.*

"I don't get it." At least the guy stood up upright again, which was something, but he was still crowding Ali's space too much for his liking. "You're one of the little guys, you're in Claude's pack. All his little guys give blowjobs when asked."

"At dinner, when there's food around?" But as Ali looked around, he could see a few blowjobs and one full out fuck going on over at the corner tables. *Wrong thing to say in Claude's club.* "It doesn't matter. I'm not in Claude's pack. I'm not a sub and just because I'm not as tall as you, does not mean I'm going to drop to my knees just because you want me to. Go away."

Shit. Another wrong thing to say. I'm batting a hundred today. The wolf's face twisted, and his fists clenched. "You've got no call to be rude to me. You made me horny. You fix it."

Ali's eyes darted right and left. He was cornered; his own fault for wanting to stay away from the masses. "I'm not being rude," he said, already calling on his animal spirit to shift. "I don't know you. I've never seen you before. I don't want to suck your dick and I'm allowed to say no." As soon as the last word was out of his mouth, Ali shifted. Wriggling through his clothes with practiced ease, he darted through the gap between the wolf's legs, and sprinted for where he last saw Claude.

It wasn't easy. Wolves loved their boots and with the big asshole shouting and trying to follow him, people were moving which made his trip more hazardous. The wooden floor was slippery under his claws, and Ali slid into a few boots, which of course made them move as well. His nerves tense, expecting any minute for a badly placed boot to land on his head, Ali chattered out a warning, but the noise level was too loud for anyone to hear. Seeing Claude's back in a sudden parting of the crowd, Ali took a chance and leapt as high as he could. His claws gripped Claude's shirt and he scurried up his friend's broad back and hid out under his hair. Chest heaving, all Ali could think was, *what the hell is that amazing smell?*

Chapter Four

As far as he was concerned, Hades had done his duty and he wanted to leave. Unfortunately, his well-meaning brother had other ideas.

"Just give this guy a chance," Sei said, leaning on Hades' shoulder. "He's little, but he's got a lot of spirit, and I don't know, I've just got a good feeling about this guy."

"Ali's been my friend for almost a hundred years." Great now Hades was being tag-teamed, with Claude chipping in his two cents worth. "He gets a lot of hassle from his scurry because of it, and he's pretty much on his own, but he's clever and sweet."

"Sweet is not a term that's going to apply to my mate, is it?" Hades caught a glimpse of what looked like a light in the far corner of the room by the food tables, but when he blinked and looked again it was gone. "Did you tell this friend of yours who I was? Did you explain how he'll have to spend time in the dreariest place across all realms, ha? No, I bet you didn't. I bet you passed me off as a friend of yours without explaining who he'd be getting mixed up with."

"He'd be good for one night..." Sei offered, but Claude scowled.

"See, that look right there. I'm not using one of Claude's friends as a one-nighter when he doesn't know who I am or hell, if he's as amazing as you say he is, what if I fall for him...?"

"What the hell?" Claude lurched forward and then reached behind his back and then up behind his neck. "Ali? Ali is that you? Are you okay? What happened? Who the hell upset you?"

Hades watched, stunned. It was as though a shaft of light beamed down from the ceiling, hitting the back of Claude's head. His heart stuttered, his breath caught, and he opened his mouth....

A huge wolf shifter stormed over, his eyes wide, his nostrils flaring. "That little rat you've got hiding in your hair, owes me a blow job."

My mate's a rat shifter? It wasn't unheard of, and Hades wasn't going to complain but….

"My *very good friend* Ali doesn't owe anyone anything, Bart, and he's not a rat," Claude snarled. "What happened? I bet I can guess. You shoved your dick in his direction and you expected him to fall all over it?"

Bart took a step back as if surprised by Claude's anger. "What's wrong with that? He's little. He made me horny."

"Doing what? Eating his meal and minding his own business, I suppose." Claude shook with anger. "I promised Ali he'd be safe here. I told him that my wolves were fucking capable of controlling themselves and wouldn't upset him. What do you call this?"

Cupping his hand carefully, Claude reached around his neck. Sitting on his palm was the cutest little chipmunk Hades had ever seen. He had pale gold fur, mixed with almost white on his belly and paws, and his face had two black streaks that ran from his sharp little eyes to the edge of his pointed ears. And he was pissed off. Sitting upright on his back legs, the little fellow jabbed his wee front legs around as though he was boxing, chattering nineteen to the dozen. Hades doubted anyone could understand what was being said, but they could understand the tone and it was all directed at the hapless Bart.

"Well, would you look at that," Sei grinned reaching out a finger as it he wanted to touch. "Ali has to be the cutest little shifter I've ever seen."

"Put your finger away," Hades muttered quietly, more to himself than anyone else. "You touch him, and I'll strip the skin from your fingers."

But obviously he wasn't quiet enough. "Brother?" Sei looked shocked and then a huge smile spread across his face. "You see the light at last?" Claude and the other wolves who'd all stood around wanting to be nosy, looked between them as if not sure what was going on.

Hades only had eyes for his cute little mate, who had stopped chattering and was now twitching his nose madly in Hades direction. "I'm not the greatest catch," he said quietly, catching the little creature's eyes, "but I'll spend eternity doing my best to make you happy if you'll let me." He slowly held out his hand and waited.

Time stood still. Hades wasn't even sure if his heart was beating anymore. The little chipmunk dropped down on all fours, looking over his shoulder at Claude who smiled, then at Bart who growled, and then back at Hades. Twitching his tail madly, he took a flying leap, landing directly on Hades' palm. Hades quickly moved his other hand to cradle him. He didn't want his little mate to fall off and hurt himself. But Ali showed no signs of falling. Looking up at Hades he pointed one of his front paws at Bart and started his angry chittering again.

"I know, I know. I completely understand." Hades said, nodding, keeping an eye on the angry shifter. "This guy has upset you and he deserves to pay. I totally agree."

"Er, bro," Sei cast a worried look in Claude's direction. "The wolves get upset when us godly beings interfere in pack affairs."

"Ali's not pack." Hades called on his power. A voice screamed in the back of his head that this was not the right place, that he could lose his mate if the wee guy couldn't handle who he was, but Hades wasn't about to shirk his duty to his precious mate on the very first day. "Do you know who I am?"

The world looked different from his new perspective. In his god form, Hades' head almost touched the ceiling – the wolves below him not even half his size. His power cloaked the room – dark, dangerous – there was not a being in existence who didn't immediately recognize how menacing he could be, even if they didn't know who he was.

Only Ali appeared unaffected. The tiny chipmunk looked even smaller in his huge hand, but the guy didn't seem worried, rubbing his cheek against Hades' thumb which Hades found rather soothing.

"I'll say again," Hades' voice bellowed around the room. "Do you know who I am and who's mate you've had the audacity to upset?"

"Oh, my gods," Bart fell to his knees, blathering. "I've done it now. My sexy shaft is going to be the death of me. That's who you are, isn't it? You're Death and you've come to take me away and fuck, I'm still hard. I can't die before I orgasm, that's just not fair."

"Actually," Thanatos pushed through the crowds, his mate tucked in by his side, "I'm Death and I'm not taking you today, although your god reference was highly accurate." He looked up at Hades and winked. "The man is a simpleton, Lord; I can see his soul. He is one of the classic examples of a man being led around by his dick, but I don't believe he meant any permanent harm to your mate."

Hades' heart almost stopped when Ali leaned over his finger, chittering madly at Thanatos. Tilting his head to one side, Thanatos listened and then nodded. "You are quite right, little one, that anger of his is a grave concern. Any of the Doms here know they have to respect the laws of consent. I'm sure Claude has a suitable punishment for him, though, don't you think? You really don't want trash like this cluttering up the Underworld."

Ali chittered a bit more and Thanatos laughed. Hades wished he had the power to understand all languages but only Death himself had been granted that power. "You're probably right about that too, little one. But the Fates get upset when someone takes a life unnecessarily and this man isn't bad, he's just misguided. I'm sure he's going to apologize, isn't he?" He looked back at Bart who was watching, his mouth slack.

"Apologize," Claude growled, stepping forward when Bart stayed silent, his fist raised. "You've upset two gods today and Death himself, not to mention my really good friend. Say you're sorry, or I'll castrate you and then we won't have to worry about your dick leading you astray again."

"Not my dick, not my dick." Bart doubled over, clutching the body part in question. "I'm sorry. I'll listen. I'll take whatever punishment you give me, but don't kill me, please don't kill me."

"It seems your presence has rendered him more useless than usual," Sei sighed, digging Hades in the thigh with his elbow. "Why don't you take your new mate somewhere special and get to know him. You have my word Bart won't bother you or your mate again."

Slowly moving his arm, Hades bought his hand up to his face. His sweet little chipmunk showed no fear – even reaching out for him with his cute front paws. "Are you ready to leave?" He asked keeping his voice as low as possible which wasn't easy in this form. Ali's excited bobbing of his head meant his fur brushed across

Hades' cheek sending tingles throughout his whole body. Closing his eyes, Hades enjoyed the sensation for just a moment, before translocating them to his favorite earthly home. No matter how accepting Ali was proving to be, he wasn't about to subject his mate to the cold hardness of the Underworld until he absolutely had to.

Chapter Five

Oh, my gods, oh, my gods. I've scored a god – an ancient god is MY mate. How cool is that, how freaking cool is that? Mother eat your heart out. This is so much better than the doctor you tried to foist me onto. And he's a man, all man. Oh, my gods. Shoots, should I even say that anymore? I have a god; I have a god as my mate. Ali barely noticed their change of location, so caught up in his good fortune. He already knew who his mate was – Hades, Lord of the Underworld - and while he knew it was probably petty of him to be so excited that others feared his mate, he couldn't help it, because *my mate's a living, breathing god.*

And it wasn't just his mate's designation that excited Ali. Hades as a god was all power and thunder, but as a man? Ali would've whimpered if he could while he was still in his fur. Tall, broad shouldered but lean, not like the muscle bound wolf who boxed him in. The first thing Ali noticed about his mate was his sensitive pale face. Light blue eyes flecked with white shone with such intensity, Ali knew in an instant he could trust the man meant to be his. The long straight nose and full lips with the cutest heart shaped dip in the middle of the top one, would have had Ali swooning at hello, if he hadn't been in his fur and pissed off at the time.

And now he was being cuddled close to a heavenly chest, long fingers holding him secure enough that his nose was full of his mate's unique scent. Ali expected a scent as dark as his mate's title, but it was light and fresh, like an olive grove in springtime. The nutty walnut undertone made Ali shiver in the most delightful way.

"Are you okay, Ali?" Hades was back to his human size. "I can take you somewhere else if you prefer?"

It would help if I knew where I was first. Ali could hear birds singing in the trees, the air was warm, but not uncomfortable – *we're not in the Underworld then.* Using one of Hades' finger for leverage, Ali wiggled himself up enough so he could see.

His mouth dropped open. A huge swathe of manicured gardens filled his eyes, the hills in the distance covered in vines, or trees of some kind. Looking around – so much green, so much life. Ali understood in an instant why this place was special to his mate. He glanced up at his mate. Hades' eyes were focused on some distant spot, giving his mate's expression a dreamy quality.

My poor mate, confined to the Underworld, when all he wants is to be among the living. All at once Ali wanted to shift and give his mate a giant hug, but he was a little unsure. For one thing, he'd be naked and while he'd love nothing more than to render Hades the same way, that was a shifter idea. Ali had no idea how a god felt about public nudity. And the public could be an issue too. Just because Ali couldn't scent anyone else close by, that didn't mean they were completely hidden from prying eyes.

And then there was that little habit of him saying what ever came into his head. Ali would admit to being impetuous at times. It was one of the reasons his scurry wanted nothing to do with him, and would turn up their snooty noses and walk away if they saw him in the street.

Maybe my fur is best for now. I can't fuck things up if he can't understand me. But it seemed Hades had a spot of mind reading talent. "Can I see you in your human form?" He asked, far more hesitantly than a god should ever be. "I can provide you clothes, shoes, whatever you want to wear."

Don't let my mouth get me into trouble, please. Not on the first day. Ali nodded, slowly and pointed to the ground. His mate was so gentle placing him on the lush grass, even though he could have easily jumped.

Thinking of his human form, Ali initiated his shift. Staying crouched, because he couldn't ignore how his cock immediately hardened, he peered at Hades from under his unruly hair. "Jeans and a shirt would be lovely, thank you. My things are still in a heap on the floor at Claude's club."

"We'll go back and get them when you're ready," Hades promised, clicking his fingers. Ali rubbed his hand over the soft shirt that was far finer than anything he'd owned before. The jeans were new, but the softer kind, not the cheap harsh denim he was used to buying, and the shiny black boots with equally shiny silver buckles were so perfect Ali fell in love with them instantly.

"You have lovely taste in clothes," Ali said, standing upright and facing his mate in his human form for the first time. "Do I pass muster?" He swallowed hard, doing a twirl so Hades couldn't see how much his reply meant to Ali.

/~/~/~/~/

Hades' mouth went dry. "Beautiful," he croaked, well aware any flirtation skills he had were totally rusted. He licked around his teeth and swallowed. "You... you...." His verbal skills deserted him. Perky was the first word that came to mind when he looked at his mate. Trim bodied, elfin-faced with a mop of hair that mimicked his animal colors – gold, white, and black loose curls creating a riot around his sweet face. Hades was drawn to his mate's lips – full and lush they were a pale shade of pink. High cheek bones and a sharply cut triangular jaw contributed to Ali's elfin features. Bright hazel eyes shone with just a hint of uncertainty.

"Just gorgeous," Hades managed to say, just in case Ali hadn't got the message. "You were created with me in mind."

"Those wacky women in Fatesville did me proud too," Ali beamed. "Look at you, all strong and sensitive like my wet dream walking."

"Sensitive?" Hades frowned. "You do know who I am, don't you?"

"Sure." Ali waved his hand, taking in Hades' frame. "You are Hades, Greek god, Lord of the Underworld, brother to Poseidon and Zeus and… and," he clapped his hand over his mouth. "Oh no, you're already married. How could I forget Persephone? You probably have kids and everything. Oh shit. Take me back, take me back to Claude's. I will not be a home wrecker. I've seen what that shit can do to people. Your story was so romantic, how you saw her and just had to have her, so you opened a huge chasm in the meadow where she was, and swept her away on your mighty chariot drawn by four giant black horses. I'm so sorry. Don't let her hate me. She'll turn me into something smelly. I'll go. You can forget you ever saw me. Shit damn and snickerdoodles. Why does this shit always happen to me?"

Hades was not impressed. There was so much wrong with Ali's cute babble he didn't know where to start. "There's no way I'm forgetting I saw you, and if you'd give me a minute to explain, you'll see why meeting you was the most wondrous thing to ever happen in my eternal life." Clicking his fingers again, he conjured up a love seat from his private sitting room. There was no way he was letting Ali live with any of the nonsense in his head for a second longer, and definitely not for the length of time it took to walk back to his house. "Sit, baby. Give me a chance to explain before you banish our mating to the annuls of the 'nevermore'."

Ali perched on the furthest end of the couch, his fingers twisting nervously in his lap. "I didn't mean to offend you, or let my mouth run off the way it did. But everyone knows the story of how you fell in love in an instant and claimed the beautiful Persephone as your own. I can't hope to compete with a goddess. I know I'm cute, but I'm not that good."

"Hush, babe," Hades shook his head. "Yes, you're definitely cute, and I'd take you over a god or goddess any day of the week. But you need to listen to me. The ancient scholars had a romanticized version of how us gods lived our lives and for some reason even modern writers continue to hang onto fictional stories from the past as if they were cast in concrete."

Ali glanced at him sideways. "Do you mean you didn't fall into insta-love with Persephone?"

"Insta-lust," Hades said firmly. "Big difference."

"But you did marry her, didn't you, so she must have meant something to you."

"Gods didn't marry as such, not like people do today. There was no ceremony or sharing of vows." Leaning back on the couch, Hades looked up at the pale blue sky awash with streaks of white clouds. "I took her down to the Underworld, and enough people witnessed the taking which is why scholars know about it today. It would have impugned Persephone's honor if I'd just had my way with her and then dumped her back at her mother's."

"You took her to bed against her will? That's... that's...." Ali sounded horrified and rightfully so.

"Not at all what you're thinking." Hades cursed the long dead scholars who twisted a tale that should never have hit the human stage. "I wined and dined that woman for a week and didn't get so much as a glimpse of her ankle. She lorded over my demons like a queen, with me scurrying along behind her begging her to favor me with just one smile."

"But the pomegranate seed?"

"Romantic nonsense." Hades let out a sigh. "Truth of the matter is, no god can enter my domain without my permission, but if they gain access, for whatever reason, there is nothing stopping them from leaving unless I do something to prevent it. You hardly think Persephone went without eating or drinking a morsel the whole week she was there, do you? She was ordering up banquets every damn night, demanding I bring in delicacies from all over the world. No, Persephone was like a mill-stone around my neck. She tasted power as a possible Queen of the Underworld, and she wasn't going to let that go without a fight. After a week, I wanted her to go. It was her that insisted on staying."

Hades was shocked when Ali started chuckling. "It wasn't funny," he said. "The whole domain used to breathe a sigh of relief when she finally started going back to her mother's."

"Tell me the sex was good at least," Ali bent over he was laughing so hard. "I've just got this picture in my head, of you the avenging lord, determined to have his wicked way with an innocent lass, and then when you capture her, she stays, and then you can't wait to get rid of her. That's hilarious."

"We never consummated our relationship," Hades bit out. That was still a sore point for him even though so much time had passed. "She preferred the pretty boys like Adonis and goodness knows how many others she took to her bed, but she never graced me with so much as a glimpse of an ankle."

"That doesn't make sense. She was your Queen, and didn't Zeus interfere decreeing she had to return to you for part of the year? Why did you...?

Surely, she...? Oh...." Understanding flashed across Ali's face.

"Exactly, my damn brother interfered so she could keep the title of Queen. Because Persephone was technically my niece, and Demeter was giving us all grief about the whole affair, he insisted she spend a third of the year with me. Every damn year and that wasn't my fault, but Persephone wasn't going to give up the title of being Queen because that gave her a higher rank than Demeter, so Zeus, thinking he was doing me a favor, insisted that meant she had to spend part of the year with me. I guess he thought she might thaw towards me over time. She never did."

"It's so strange," Ali said. "I mean, I believe you, but all of the stories about the abduction tell of the grief Demeter felt when you kept her daughter and how the world suffered a terrible drought because she was so cut up about it."

"Yes, Demeter made it all about her, which was typical. The stories never said anything about how Persephone reacted to being abducted, or how it was her that insisted she be Queen and rule by my side. All the stories focused on Demeter's grief and how she punished the world because of it, to the point Zeus decided to step in. I was the big bad lord of the Underworld, who clearly couldn't get a date any other way. It makes me sick to think about it." Hades didn't mean to sound so bitter, but the situation still rankled on his last nerve. It was all Zeus's fault. It was him that told Hades that a grand gesture would secure him a quick roll in the bed sheets with a pretty girl. That was one mistake Hades had been paying for ever since.

"Well, you did abduct her so you could have your way with her," Ali said. "She must have meant something to you at the time."

"I was lonely," Hades admitted. "For a while, I thought that having someone around, even if it was a woman who never gave me a favorable glance would make things better. But instead, she told Hercules he could take Cerberus, she interfered with a whole stack of other affairs that had absolutely nothing to do with her. And to top it all off, she got pissed off when I did find a woman who would happily share her bed with me, and turned her into a mint plant because she was so jealous."

"Sounds like a surreal episode from Marriages from Hell. That had to suck."

Hades nodded, then turned his head to look at his mate. "You do believe me, don't you? Persephone stopped adhering to her four month visits centuries ago. She only turns up now if she wants something and that's very rare. If you claimed me, you would be the true ruler by my side, although I have to confess the Underworld is not the nicest of places."

The smile Ali gave him was like a brush of sunshine. "I'm not going to meddle in stuff that doesn't have anything to do with me and I'm not going to run away from you now I know the true story. I just don't believe that anyone has the right to come between partners in marriage. Vows are important and shouldn't be discarded or forgotten just because someone younger or sexier comes along."

"You are a good man, and you have a sweet soul." Hades smiled.

"I just have one teensy, tiny, question," Ali said, shuffling closer. Hades' heart thumped a little faster. "You've talked about your wife and your mistress, but have you ever had a male lover before? Because, you know, not everyone's cut out for man sex, and I don't want to upset you, or do something you don't enjoy. Then there's the whole stigma thing. Oh, it's gotten better in some places here on earth, but are you going to be okay when your family realizes you're gay, even if it is just for me?"

Raising his arm, Hades patted the empty space beside him. Ali slid across the extra inches between them. The heat from Ali's body made Hades feel things he believed dormant in himself. "Most gods don't worry about things like gender," he said loving how Ali tucked so readily into his side. "Why should that be important, when it's our souls that connect with each other? There will be some who might make their opinions known, but one of the benefits of being the 'invisible' god, is that no one really gives a damn what I do. And yes, I've had sex with males – a few of them in Claude's club in fact."

Shit I probably shouldn't have mentioned that. "I guess I was drawn to the place, even though I didn't know why. Now I know it was because of you." Hades forced his lips into a smile as he looked down at his mate.

"Hmm." Ali's face screamed of disapproval, but then just as quickly he beamed. "Guess it's good I'm not a virgin either, although I wouldn't know what to do with women's bits without a full color manual."

He tilted his head and Hades wondered what he was thinking. *Hopefully soon I will know.*

"You do know if you claim me, you can't get hard for anyone else again, don't you? It's got something to do with when a shifter bites their mate, which they have to do to claim them. Not that I'm assuming you're going to let me bite you anytime soon, but that is a pretty big side effect for someone who swings both ways. I don't have any squishy bits."

You can't expect him to trust you yet, even so, Hades felt a bit hurt that Ali worried he'd still be lusting after women, even after they were claimed. But the small white tooth appearing on the side of Ali's lips told a different story. Someone had made Ali feel as though he'd never be good enough. Tamping down the anger, Hades reached around and effortlessly swung Ali onto his lap.

"All the gods know that if they mate with a shifter, their dick won't work for anyone else," he said gravely, resting his hands around Ali's back.

"Poseidon made such a stink about it when he let Claude bite him, I'm sure they're still talking about it down in Tartarus. Zeus won't go within a mile of anyone furry in case one of them turns out to be his mate. It's probably one of the reasons he didn't attend the wedding, although he's a stuck up snob too, and that might have had something to do with it."

"But I've always been different," Hades willed his mate to understand. "I've been looking for you, actively looking, lurking around every pack, pride, and herd I could find."

"You wanted a shifter for a mate?" Ali's eyes reflected his confusion. "But you're the mighty Hades. You could have anyone you wanted."

"They wouldn't have wanted me." Hades tried to hide his bitterness, but memories of Persephone's scorn still rankled. "Gods are notoriously fickle – that part of ancient lore is unfortunately true. Being cast as the black sheep of the family doesn't help."

"Then there's something wrong with your family's sense of loyalty." Ali reached for him, much like he did in his furry form, but this time Hades could truly savor the warmth of his mate's hand on the side of his jaw. "Any one only has to look into your eyes to know you're a good man."

Hades' heart skipped a beat. *He's telling the truth as he sees it, and by all that's precious I want to believe him.* "Then you see more than they ever have. But just imagine, if the Fates had tied my threads to another god, like my nephew found with his mate Silvanus. The Underworld... fidelity... the reputation of the gods themselves... I wanted my mate to be a shifter. I needed that certainty."

"You'll have that with me. I would never stray. I'm just not built that way."

The words were true, Hades didn't doubt it. But from the way his mate worried his bottom lip, Hades got the impression Ali was holding something back. "What is it? Have you got something else to tell me? Surely you know mates can share anything with each other?"

"You're going to regret saying that," Ali replied with a tilt of his head and rueful grin. "My mouth tends to work before my brain half the time, and I'm not known for being subtle. I was trying to behave myself, seeing as we'd only just met."

"That's sweet of you, but totally unnecessary. You tend to develop a thick skin when you're in my line of work. Now what is it? What are you holding back?"

Ali searched his face, a whole myriad of emotions fluttering through his eyes. But then he nodded, his lips tight, and Hades wondered if he was ready to hear what his mate had to say.

Chapter Six

"I'm pissed off, okay?" Once Ali started, he knew it was going to all come pouring out. "Not at you, never at you," he added quickly when the Lord of the Underworld flinched – *see, that's just proving my point about keeping my big lips sewed together.*

"It's okay," Hades' voice was quiet. "Say what you need to say."

"I don't think you've done anything wrong." Unable to sit still, Ali shuffled off his mate's lap, and started pacing in front of the couch. "I'm so mad I could scream. No one understands you, do they?" He waved a hand in Hades direction but didn't wait for a reply. "No one stops to think what a shit job you ended up with, but you took it for more time than I can comprehend."

Hades murmured something but Ali wasn't listening.

"Persephone is a classic example – do not get me started on her. If I ever see her, I'll pull her fucking blond strands out of her empty skull. How dare she treat you like you don't matter. How dare she stomp around your domain like she owns it for all time just because you had the hots for her once. She didn't put out. She never bothered to commit herself to you. She doesn't deserve anything, but because you're a good person, with a good soul, you let your younger brother interfere in your affairs all because he won the celestial coin toss. It fucking sucks!"

"Why should you be cast as the bad one? The one everyone avoids or fears." Ali was trembling, he was so angry. Facing his mate, he yelled, "You've got a loving soul, otherwise you'd never have brought me to this beautiful place. So, tell me, why? What would have happened that day you guys were divvying up the domains? What would have happened if you'd gotten the sea, or Zeus's lofty clouds – would the rest of the grand poobah's still treat you as though you were nothing? Someone has to do your job; someone has to make sure the evil spirits don't wreak havoc on earth, and you got the short straw. That doesn't make you a bad person."

"It just makes me so damn angry." Ali's heart was racing so fast he thought it'd pop out of his chest. "You didn't whine, you haven't complained. Even when Persephone treated you like shit, you just took it like the awesome man you are. But I don't get it. Why wouldn't that she-bitch sleep with you? Hasn't she got eyes? I mean look at you. You're hot with a capital H and yeah, so you might have gone a bit caveman on her, but fuck everyone was doing that type of thing back then. And yeah, okay, I might have a spot of the green-eyed monster going on, but you're perfect and she... he... they had no right!"

Ali stood, panting, his chest heaving hard enough to hurt, his cock pushing just as hard against the front of his pants. "I hate that you've spent all this time alone just because I hadn't been born yet," he said in a quieter tone this time. "I hate that when I die, you're going to be alone all over again with a broken heart and no one to hug you. You deserve so much better – you deserve so much better than me. But I'm what you've ended up with."

He couldn't even look at Hades. The poor man was probably thinking of psych wards even now, looking for somewhere to dump him in. Any moment, Ali expected to be whisked off in a blaze of cells, probably back to where his clothes were at Claude's. So, when he was lifted off his feet, and his mouth was suddenly covered with a warm and questing set of lips, Ali might have been a bit slow to react. In his mind he was wondering how he'd look in a straight-jacket – not good.

But he caught on fast. Clinging like a spider monkey, Ali reached up, one arm hooked around Hades' neck, his other hand buried in his mate's short black hair. When Hades' tongue pressed against his lips, Ali opened his mouth willingly. Hades possessed him like a fire storm. Every part of his body responded. His heart pumped his blood south, his lungs filled as though they'd burst and still Ali couldn't let go. His hips had taken on a life of their own, humping against Hades' cloth covered length, but it wasn't just his hips. Ali wanted to get closer, needed every inch of his body pressed against his mate's. Writhing, pressing, wriggling in Hades' tight grip, he was about ready to climax when Hades finally pulled back so he could breathe.

"No, don't stop." Ali tugged on Hades neck.

"Sweetheart," Hades was panting, his pupils blown. "I was going to at least get you dinner first, seeing as yours was interrupted."

"Feed me afterwards." Ali thought there might have been some growling involved, which for a chipmunk was rare, but Hades got the hint. *Gods these kisses are sinfully hot.*

/~/~/~/~/

Hades never intended to pull a caveman act, Ali's words, not his. After all, the one time he had done that, he'd been given nothing but an eternity of grief. But there was something in the way Ali defended him, even got jealous over him and events that happened way before his little mate was born, that set a match to the kindling of Hades' heart and he couldn't help himself.

"I don't have words for how happy I am you're mine," he managed to pant out when they broke for air again. Ali gave all the signs of being a determined chipmunk because it was his lips that were taken before he had a chance to say anything else.

And who needed words? Their bodies were shouting enough intent for Zeus to hear, and wasn't that the point? He had his mate in his arms, a mate who would never stray, never look at him as though he was something the dog dragged in. Ali defended him, cared for him already, and Hades' empty soul lapped up the attention faster than a brittle sponge thrown into the sea.

Where to go? What...? Hades couldn't think straight. He wanted nothing more than to lie his mate down in the lush grass and rut until they both came, then strip him out of his restrictive clothing and do it all over again. But this was a claiming and his sweet mate deserved more than sticky jeans for his troubles. *I need to focus* – because translocating without it was a ridiculous thing to do.

Ali's kisses made focusing damn near impossible. Somehow, his sweet mate had got his pants undone. One hand semi-circling around the head of his cock, and Hades yanked his lips away from his mate's and cried out as his hips instinctively thrust forward. His balls pulsing harder than they ever had, it was all Hades could do to keep them upright. It was glorious, amazing, but nowhere near enough.

He and Ali were on the same page. "Find us a bed, big guy," Ali panted. "Quick, before my ass combusts."

Hades held up one finger. *Hold on just a minute. Come on brain.* "Did you... can I...?"

"I came, but that was only the warmup act."

Thank fuck. Hades was only dimly aware of the air around them swirling as he translocated them to his master bedroom. Magic had its uses. By the time they'd landed on his soft feather covers they were both naked.

"Damn, you look amazing." Ali scrambled around, straddling Hades' hips, his pert ass cradling Hades' cock which was still hard. "Hmm, look at all this skin." His fingers were as busy as his eyes.

Hades felt his cheeks heat up, something that never happened, but there was another part of him that gloried at being the focus of so much loving attention. *How long has it been?* Hades discounted the young men he'd fucked at Claude's. None of them had taken the initiative, or had so much fun doing so.

Ali was in a completely different class. Hades groaned as hot lips circled his tight nipples and sucked. He reached out, holding Ali's hips still as the man threatened to cause him to blow a second time by wiggling his cute ass as he moved his head from one nip to the next. There was a part of Hades that could imagine him laying like a king and just letting his mate work his wondrous lips over every inch of his body again and again. But his cock had very definite other ideas.

And so did Ali. "Can you do your magic finger thingy like Sei does to Claude?" He asked, sitting upright, totally unconcerned about his nudity. Hades was too busy taking in the slender tanned frame to understand the question at first. A slap to his chest made him notice. "You're a big guy in every department," Ali gave another wiggle and Hades groaned. *I'm so close, again!* "Are you magicking or fingering my ass open?"

"Magic." Hades didn't have the patience for anything else, or the staying power. One thought, and he knew his mate could take him easily, but as he pondered decisions on positions, Ali took care of that too.

"There's something really hot about sitting on a thick cock," Ali muttered as he lifted up, grabbed Hades' cock and did exactly that. "So... em... hot.... Damn I said that already. Fuck... you're big... but oh... so good." He let out a long satisfied sigh as his butt kissed the top of Hades' thighs.

Hades froze. He'd barely had the chance to relish the feeling of his cock pushing into willing flesh, but now that same cock was caught in a hot, pulsing vice that was tugging on every sensual nerve in his body. One move and he'd have the shortest claiming in history. Reaching up, he coaxed Ali's head down, arching his own neck so he could steal a kiss.

"Don't move," he whispered as their lips met. "Please. Don't move a single freaking inch."

Ali's smirk was obvious, but he did as Hades asked, holding his lower body still as their hands moved languidly over naked skin and their lips nipped and sucked at each other. Hades tried desperately to think of anything else except the fact that his cock was deep inside his mate's most intimate place.

It was a pointless task. Every urge ordered him to flip Ali over and pound into him, staking the most primitive of claims. And Ali wasn't helping matters. Every little whimper, sharp inhale, and deep moan called to Hades' inner core – a sexual beast he didn't know existed. Hades knew if he didn't do something, he'd be spilling inside his mate without a single thrust.

"Please." Ali wiggled again. "Let me move, damn it."

Hades lost it. Holding Ali tight, he rolled them both over, catching Ali's knees with his arms, and thrusting his hips hard. Ali yelled, but he was doing his best to push back with his butt, and his slender cock had an angry red tip that leaked as it bounced over his abdomen. Keeping Ali's legs spread, and his ass tipped up, Hades punched his fists into the mattress to anchor himself, and let his body move in a rhythm as old as time itself.

There was no music, no celestial bards singing about the virtues of love and togetherness for all time. The only sounds were slapping skin, harsh panting, moans from Ali, and grunts which Hades realized were coming from him. He wanted, he needed to be so deep inside his mate that no one would ever doubt his claim. The ass he was pounding was his for all time, and it would be all time, because as Hades' body tightened, and the ache in his lower abs grew into a roar, he reached up with his right hand and cupped Ali's neck.

"*Meus in sempiternum*," he cried out, the skin under his palm heating as he marked his mate forever, inside and out.

Ali stilled, then cried out, splashes of spunk coating his abs as his body shuddered and twitched. Two cute little fangs shot down over his lower lip and Hades leaned over, using the hand he'd claimed with to tug Ali's head closer. "Bite me!" There might have been shades of the Underworld Lord in his tone, but if there was, Ali didn't notice. He latched onto Hades' neck; Hades felt a sharp pinch and then his body was flooded with even more endorphins as his body threw him into another orgasm.

Hades couldn't move if his life depended on it. He was wiped out, totally exhausted, and yet there was an energy pulsing through him, making him feel as though he could fight a dozen demons with one hand tied behind his back. He looked down as the pressure on his neck eased. A few licks and Ali flopped back on the bed. His face was red and shone with sweat, but his eyes were glowing. Hades got the impression both man and chipmunk were pleased with themselves.

"Are you going to let go of my legs anytime soon?" Ali asked with a tired grin. "And maybe you could poof up that dinner you promised me, and possibly do some magic handwaving cleaning up thingy 'cos I'm too lazy to move?"

Hades traced the mark he'd left on Ali's neck – the black two pronged spear and a dangling key. The join between his own neck and shoulder tingled where Ali had marked him in return. "Are you going to boss me for eternity?" he teased, praying it would be so.

"Only on the things that matter." Ali's contented smile gave Hades the energy he needed to move.

Chapter Seven

"Ooh, what are those shiny orb thingies?" Ali bounced into the kitchen, fully refreshed after what could only be called the "BEST" night of his life, to find his new mate showing remarkable skill with a frying pan.

"Messages from my P.A." Hades sounded a little short, but he accepted Ali's non-verbal request for a kiss easily. "Sit down, my sweet. Breakfast will be ready in an instant."

"I do love breakfast," Ali beamed, sliding into the handy kitchen chair. "I think a breakfast sets you up for the rest of the day, don't you?"

"I enjoy it when I can." Hades tipped the contents of the frying pan onto a platter and then bent over, taking something out of the oven. Resting his chin on the palm of his hand, Ali allowed himself a silent drool. Even dressed in dour black without a hair out of place, his mate was worth looking at.

"I wasn't sure what you'd enjoy," Hade said, coming over to the table with his hands and arms full of platters. "I made pancakes, waffles, and toast. There's plenty of bacon, sausages, eggs fried and scrambled, and hash browns. I also whipped up some oatmeal just in case you preferred porridge to start your day."

He set the different dishes on the table. All Ali could do was stare.

"If there's something I've forgotten, just let me know and I'll get it for you instantly. It's always difficult, with a new person, knowing what you might like."

"You did…." Ali swallowed and tried again. "You did all this for me? How long have you been awake?"

"Not long," Hades sat in the chair opposite. But for some reason, he wouldn't meet Ali's eyes. "I did a quick search on what chipmunks ate in the wild, to try and help with breakfast ideas, but I didn't think you'd be keen on worms. There are nuts and berries in the oatmeal though."

"I can eat anything, except worms." Ali shuddered. "But babe, why didn't you wake me up? I could've helped you. I'm not bad in the kitchen."

"You didn't get dinner." Hades lifted his shoulder, some sort of a shrug Ali supposed. "You should eat up. We don't want it getting cold."

"I'm sure you could heat it up for us with a wave of your godly hand." Ignoring the plates, although the food did smell wonderful, Ali reached over, grabbing Hades' hand as he was reaching for a plate. "Babe, what's wrong? Are you having claiming remorse?"

"What? No." Ali found his hand clasped between Hades'. At least his mate was looking at him now. "I just wanted to do something nice for you. As a god, I'm not very useful for much unless you have any enemies you want me to scare to death. Cooking for someone is supposed to be a nice thing to do."

"It's a wonderful thing to do," Ali said quickly. *Oh, my poor mate, you've got a severe case of insecurity.* "Can I say something, and I don't want you to take offense?"

Hades nodded.

Hmm, how to put this. "Hades," Ali said firmly, "I'm not Persephone. For one thing I don't have the hair, or the goddess powers, nor am I blessed with womanly curves. But one of the key differences, between her and me, is that I care a lot for you already. You rocked my world last night, three times. I carry your mark on my neck and wear it proudly. We're mates – true mates and as your mate, I don't want to hear you running yourself down, saying your only skill is to scare someone... not that that wouldn't be handy on occasion, but Hades you are so much more than that."

"Down there, maybe." Hades tilted his head to the floor, "but here on earth I make grown men shiver and cower with fear, and that's it. I should've taken you out somewhere nice for breakfast, but I didn't want you to see that side of life with me so soon."

That's soooo sad. Without thinking, Ali snatched back his hand and scrambled off his chair, hurrying around the table and wiggling his way onto Hades' lap. One hand resting around Hades' neck, Ali leaned forward and snatched an extra crispy piece of bacon off the plate. Holding it up to Hades' lips, he got a warm glow of pleasure when his mate took it and started chewing.

"I don't give a hairy shit what other people think about you, my mate," Ali said, snagging a hash brown and taking a bite, before offering the rest to Hades. Crisp flavors burst across his tongue, and on any normal day Ali would've dived right in, but he had a mate to reassure. "I figure, if people are scared of you, and they know who you are, then that simply means they've got a guilty conscience and are worried you're going to be punishing their spirit one day. Anyone who has a clear conscience isn't going to be afraid of a few heebie jeebies."

"But that's what I do – it's who I am. I'm responsible for setting up the punishments for the evil spirits I get sent. You can't do that if you're a nice person."

Well, aren't you stubborn in the mornings. Ali picked up another rasher of bacon and fed it to his mate before getting one for himself. "As I understand it, that's part of your job description," he said between chews. "People do evil things, and that shuts them out of whatever heaven they believe in. I am guessing they get sent to you because they can't be around decent dead people and you punish them, with a torture that fits their crimes because there has to be consequences for their actions."

"Their torture doesn't make any difference to the people those evil doers have wronged. And what does that say about me, that I'm the one to set their punishment?"

"You're a man with a difficult job." Reaching over, Ali dragged the plate of scrambled eggs closer and picked up a fork. "Open wide."

Hades made a sound that was suspiciously like a chortle, but he opened his mouth anyway and for a while the two men worked their way through the dish of eggs, one mouthful at a time.

"You know, the way I see it, and correct me if I'm wrong," Ali said once the plate was almost empty. "I think souls know. I think there's some instinct, some sense of knowing, even when we die badly, although is there any good way?"

Ali thought for a moment, distracted by the idea, and then remembered his original point. "This whole thing about consequences. If someone dies a horrible death at the hands of an evil person for example, then that victim is never going to know if the evil person is caught, or made to pay for their sins. They're dead. But, I'm sure there's a part of our spiritual side that believes in some form of cosmic justice, even if it's purely on a sub-conscious level."

"Not if they're agnostic." Hades shook his head at the forkful of eggs Ali offered, and picked up a sausage instead. Leaning forward, because Ali wasn't going to not share such a delicious treat, Ali took a quick bite and followed it with the forkful of egg.

"I don't think religion matters in that respect," Ali said when he'd swallowed. "I mean, there must be hundreds of religions in the world."

"Over four thousand at last count."

"Shazba, that's a lot." Ali was momentarily distracted again. Watching Hades eat a sausage with his fingers, was the best kind of food porn. "Anyway," he said, when Hades popped the last bit in his mouth, "regardless of religion, or what you believe happens when you die, everyone believes in consequences, right? Otherwise, everyone would just run around like fiends and do whatever the hell they liked when they were living. But we don't, because we don't want bad shit happening to us as a consequence."

"You also have a lot of laws that are a good deterrent," Hades pointed out. "Humans and paranormals are not intrinsically bad, just the same as any other living species. It's not possible for a person to be born bad. Every spirit that emerges in a newborn has a pure white soul." Hades offered a piece of toast which Ali took and nibbled on. His stomach was letting him know he was getting quite full, but feeding his mate, and being fed was surprisingly intimate, even if the conversation was serious.

"But then life happens, and we all stuff up to various degrees." Ali stopped. He couldn't remember the point he was originally trying to make. *Oh, that's right. My mate thinks his job makes him a bad person.* "Anyhow, the point I was trying to make is that just because you set up tortures and punishments for bad spirits, I think you're doing a good thing. On a cosmic level, you're providing justice for those who's voices won't be heard. Because, they're dead," he added in case Hades didn't quite get his point. "And dead people can't speak, at least on earth. So you see, you're doing a good thing, in a bad way, but it's not bad, if you see my point."

"I think you're incredibly sweet, and I thank you for not thinking badly about who I am or what I do," Hades said, and Ali would swear the man's eyes were kind even if no one else could see it but him. They both looked over to the kitchen counter where another orb dinged as it appeared.

"Do those shiny things mean another person has died?" Ali asked.

"Good gracious, no," Hades shook his head, and yep, Ali was sure he saw the glimmerings of a smile. "Did you know, around the world, approximately one hundred people die every single minute. I mean, it's offset because roughly two hundred and fifty people are born every minute too, but if I had a notification for every time a spirit entered my realm, we'd be buried in orbs in the time it took to eat breakfast."

"So, what are they? And why are they appearing here, wherever here is?"

"They're message orbs, my sweet precious, which means my PA is getting in a flap." Hades dropped a kiss on his head, which Ali thought was such a sweet gesture. "As to where we are, this is my estate in Greece. How about we ignore the orbs for now and I'll show you around?"

"We're in Greece, actual Greece, the country?" *So exciting. I don't even own a passport.* "Are you sure it's okay to ignore your PA for a bit? If he's in a flap, he might need your help."

"Folsom is always getting in a flap, so yep, we've got time." Hades' arm curled around him, and his head bent. Ali tilted his face up. Kissing was far better than listening to the orbs and their annoying ding and Ali didn't want to go anywhere until he'd had a chance to appreciate his mate's Greek estate. *I can't believe I'm in Greece.*

Chapter Eight

My mate is like a breath of sunshine and fresh air all rolled into one. Hades had always loved his earthly home, but seeing it through Ali's eyes was as though the whole place had been painted in technicolor. Ali was so intensely interested in the information his workers shared – Hades provided the translation services – and for the first time ever, those workers didn't seem to have a problem with him around. Usually, they all ducked their heads and suddenly had something to do when Hades came into sight. But thanks to Ali, those same workers were now showing him how the press worked, how to tell when olives were totally ripe and ready for picking, and all sorts of information Ali would never need or use, but he lapped it all up any way.

That boundless curiosity extended to the house too. His sweet mate was fascinated with the bits and bobs Hades had around the house. Hades had always been an ardent collector of the unusual, and many of his items were thousands of years old, but they were just as likely to share space with the latest sculpture from local artists. Ali chatted incessantly, asking questions with a huge smile on his face all the while. It warmed Hades' very soul to be bathed in the glow of his mate's smile and the positive feelings that stemmed from other people around them.

But as the day moved on, the tiny pool of agitation in Hades' stomach grew into a cesspool. He'd managed to forestall the inevitable by cooking lunch, but now the table was cleared, and Ali was looking at him expectantly.

"We need to get down to the Underworld, don't we?" Ali's eyes were shiny, and his nose was red from where it'd caught in the sun. "How do we do this? Is it just another translocation thingy?"

"I was thinking, maybe...." Hades inhaled sharply. "Maybe you could stay here. I'll only be gone an hour or two at the most, and then when I get back…."

"Oh, no, mister, you are not leaving me here." The glare Ali gave him froze Hades to his seat. "You even think of trolling down to your world without me, and you'll be sleeping on the couch for a damn week."

Hades' heart sank. "Babe, precious, sweetheart, the Underworld is not a nice place. It's black, and dark, and cold, and full of horrible people, demons and hellhounds. I don't want to see your bright spirit dragged down by all the stuff I have to do, or the beings I have to deal with."

Ali crossed his arms over his chest. His lips were a tight line.

"I don't want anything to happen to you," Hades said desperately. "You're good and kind and sweet…."

"And feisty, strong willed and a loyal chipmunk who'll go with his mate to the ends of the earth and beyond if necessary," Ali interrupted sharply. "The Underworld is your home, the realm you command with all in it. Are you telling me when you thought of meeting your mate, you expected your mate to stay topside, while you slogged through the drudgery of the Underworld alone? Do you honestly expect me to stay here, and just wait on you to come around when you have time for a booty call?"

Ali's voice was rising, and Hades wasn't stupid. "Sweetheart, I'd never thought of a mating like that. It's just…."

"Just nothing!" Ali punched the tabletop as he stood up, his lips pursed and his eyebrows low over his eyes. "You told me I would rule by your side. You told me how lonely you were when you went down there. You were the one who told me how you needed the certainty of having a shifter mate. Well, guess what, bucko. You got one. And if you think any mate worth their fur would let their mate drown in the misery and sorrow of the Underworld alone, then you'd better get a brain reset."

Hades slumped back in his chair. He knew when he was beat. "You're going to hate me," he said, almost in a whisper. "You're going to hate me, and my realm, and...."

"Oh, no, no, no, no, no." All the anger in Ali's body visibly drained away. He was around the table and on Hades' lap before Hades could blink. "I could never hate you," Ali whispered, and Hades was shocked to see tears in his eyes. "Going down there just allows me to see the other side of you, that's all. Hades, my mate, the Underworld is never going to go away, or at least I hope it doesn't because simply having somewhere like the Underworld where the evil spirits can be kept away from others is a good thing. And ruling that realm is a huge part of who you are. You can't shut me away from that."

"I didn't want to shut you away from that side of me indefinitely," Hades said. "We've only just met. We haven't had time to get to know each other or...."

"I'm not going to know the real you until I've seen you in your home realm."

Ali was right. Hades knew that, but even beings like Thanatos were never sure what to make of him and Death had lived in the Underworld as long as Hades had. He looked around the bright and cheery kitchen, painted in whites and yellows and mentally compared it to the cold starkness of his home in his realm. The thought of his bright and precious Ali shining like a globe in all that gloom made him shiver. But Hades wasn't ready to risk his mating at such an early stage by leaving Ali behind.

"I'll take you," he said even as his heart sunk at the thought. "I'll take you, but you have to promise me one thing. You must never, ever, ever, tell anyone down there your full name. Do you promise me? It's really important."

"I don't usually use my full name with anyone unless I'm applying for a job. But why? Why is it so important no one in the Underworld knows it?"

"Names have incredible power," Hades said gravely. "Every demon knows that if someone learns their birth name, then they can be summoned, and controlled for nefarious reasons. I'm not saying it's possible someone can summon you. I'm not sure. But if any of my demons thought you could be, and they learned your name and sold or bartered it for something else, they could try. You could get hurt."

Ali opened his mouth, probably to argue, and Hades hardened his stare. After a long minute, Ali nodded. "You have my word no one will know my full name, even if they try and torture it out of me."

Oh, my fucking stars. Hades hadn't even thought of that. But the time for talking was done. Another three orbs were cluttering up the kitchen counter just in the time they were arguing about Ali going. Hades was going to give Folsom a stern talking to about overusing the communication devices when he got back.

This had better be bloody important, he thought as he held tight to his mate and whisked them down to his throne room.

/~/~/~/~/

The first thing that struck Ali as unusual was how light it was in Hades' Underworld home, which was surprising in itself because everything around was black – the walls, the ceiling, even the marble on the floor was black. There was a fire pit, throwing out heaps of heat into the room, but the flames were the only color.

The second thing that struck him, as he looked around was how silent it was. Ali had had a stern pep talk with his inner diva and his chipmunk on how they were going to have to get used to the sound of screams before Hades transported them. He was trying to be logical and well-prepared. No one getting tortured were ever silent about it.

But Ali couldn't hear anything, not so much as a whimper. "Er…," he asked hesitantly, "are the demons having a lunch break or something? Only, I can't hear a thing."

"The torture rings are a long way from the house and these walls are soundproofed." Hades was looking at the stage his throne was on. At least Ali guessed it was Hades' throne. He didn't know anyone else who'd sit on a chair made entirely of bones. He jumped when a slightly smaller one appeared next to the original, but then the corner of his lips twitched up. His throne had a bright red cushion on it. *My mate is so good to me.*

"So, where are we exactly?" Ali twirled around taking in the huge ceilings that were at least fifty feet above his head. "Is this where you make all your godly decisions? Or did you just bring me here first, so we didn't have to see anyone?"

He looked down at his black pants and bright pink t-shirt. They were smarter than anything he'd owned before, but it wasn't a consort outfit. "Should I have changed into something else? Is there a dress code down here? Are you going to shut me in here while you go and see what Folsom wants, or...."

"This is the seat of my power, where I interview demons, the damned souls, and occasionally my PA," Hades interrupted gently. Ali found himself being led over to the smaller throne. "Folsom needs to learn to not keep bugging me when I'm on earth, and calling him in here so I can speak to him about it, sends a message far more effective than words."

"That's very clever thinking." Ali wriggled in his seat. The cushion helped but the bones in the back of the throne still pressed into his back. "Do you have to be in here very often? Only these seats are not the most comfortable. How on earth do you put up with it?"

"Have another cushion." Another one, bright red just like the first, appeared on Ali's lap. "I'm used to it."

O-kay. Leaning forward, Ali stuffed the cushion behind his back. It did help.

"When I'm down here, especially in this room, I have to be the God my demons fear, otherwise they'd run amuck, and I'd have hell on my hands."

Ali figured a tortured spirit would figure this place was hell even on a good day. But he didn't understand the nuances of the different facets of the afterlife, and from the look on Hades' face, now was not the time to ask.

"As my consort, I need you to not react, not flinch, or anything else that might be a sign of weakness, no matter what I say or do. Can you do that for me?"

Oh, sugar snaps, what have I got myself into? Ali nodded. Hades' hand in his was a nice touch, and it helped. But slowly the room got colder. Ali could feel Hades' power increase although he retained his human form. Ali was glad about the human size of things. Next to Hades' true god form, he'd look like an ant.

"Folsom." Hades didn't yell, he didn't even raise his voice, but it was as if his single word thundered around the room. Even the walls rippled, and the marble floor tiles moved like a wave, up and down. There was a scrabbling of feet by the huge doors Ali only just noticed, and a bright green, *was that a demon*, came running in, stumbling in his haste to prostrate himself on the floor in front of the throne.

"My Lord Hades," Folsom, because it couldn't be anyone else, said dramatically. "You bellowed?" The effect was muffled somewhat as Folsom was speaking into the floor, but the demon still managed to show off some attitude. Ali wanted to smile, but he wouldn't do anything to upset his mate's moment.

"Twenty seven communication orbs in six hours, Folsom. Explain yourself." Hades' voice was hard and unflinching, but Ali felt a warmth in his groin. He'd always been a sucker for a masterful man.

"Can I get up?"

"No."

"Fine then. The first four orbs were me asking if your brother and his consort had liked the gift I selected and spent hours wrapping for them." Folsom waited, Ali waited, but Hades didn't say anything.

"The next two orbs were to remind you to call Queen Persephone, because she can be a bitch when you ignore her and I'm the one who has to...."

"That's only six of the twenty seven orbs," Hades cut in.

"Fine, right. Well, then I was getting a bit worried, because that damn dog of yours hadn't been fed, and his whines and howls could be heard all over the court. You know he won't take his food from anyone else which means...."

Hades has a dog? Ali felt the warm glow in his pants increase, until he remembered the stories about Cerberus. Having three heads didn't sound as cute as the mental picture he'd got in his head about Hades playing with puppies.

"He was fed before I went to the wedding. After him trying to take over my realm and almost killing my nephew Lasse to do it, he's lucky I don't starve him to death."

"Yes, my Lord. That is your right, my Lord." Ali got the impression Folsom said those words in the same placating tone quite often, which wasn't surprising given how hard Hades was being.

"Are you telling me all of the other orbs were to do with that damn dog?"

"No, my Lord." Folsom sat up even though Hades hadn't said he could. Ali caught him flicker a glance his way, but for the most part his attention was on Hades. "Your brother Poseidon saw fit to let Zeus know about you finding your fated mate. Congratulations, by the way, even if you haven't introduced me yet. The rest of the orbs were to ask you to get your godly ass down here, because Demeter found out about your mate from Zeus, and of course, that meant Persephone found out from her, because Mommy dearest

118

couldn't wait to tell her darling daughter she'd been replaced in your affections. The upshot of it is, Persephone demands entrance at the gates at ten am tomorrow and she's not taking no for an answer. I told you, you should have called her."

Hades groaned, and Ali had a strong feeling his mate needed a nice long hug. It was a shame the thrones were so damned uncomfortable.

Chapter Nine

Why does my past have to come back and bite me in the ass at precisely the wrong moment? Hades' first instinct, on learning that Persephone was visiting, was to just spirit himself and Ali back to Greece, or maybe Claude's, the Virgin Islands, or even Alaska. Basically, anywhere Persephone wasn't. But that wouldn't be fair to Folsom, the Hellhounds, the house demons, or the demon supervisors who ran his torture chambers. They shouldn't have to fear her wrath just because he was playing chicken.

But maybe he could…. "Ali, mate of mine, there's no need for you to be here when…."

"We've had this discussion, Hades." Yep, Ali was back to being stubborn. "Now, if we're having visitors is there anything we need to prepare for when she gets here? Special foods to be ordered in? or is there a room she prefers to sleep in? Is she staying, or is this just a brief visit?" Hades looked up to see Ali was looking at Folsom, not him.

"We weren't even staying here tonight ourselves," Hades protested. "I thought you wanted to go to Claude's to get your clothes. Aren't you worried about your phone, your keys, or your wallet, or something?"

"Claude will keep them safe for me and why wouldn't I want to stay here?" Ali looked around and shrugged. "This place needs a bit of color, maybe not this room because you have to be your impressive self in here and I'm sure the black walls and oversized firepit add to the ambience necessary for a place like this. If your living quarters are decked out in the same black, then you and I can discuss making some changes. But we can worry about that later. Now, Folsom, isn't it? What else do we do when a visiting goddess arrives?"

"Try and stay out of her way, as a rule," Folsom glanced at Hades seeking his approval to speak. Hades just waved his hand for his PA to continue. His mated life was already going down the drain anyway. His PA couldn't do much more damage.

"Well," Folsom focused back on Ali, bristling like the gossip he was. "Usually when the mistress visits, Hades greets her at the gate, 'cos she can't get in otherwise, and then they walk back to the house, firstly, because the mistress likes to throw out a few insults at the guards, the hounds, and usually Cerberus too, and secondly because she swore blind she'd never ride in Hades' carriage again. By the time they get to the house, the arguments have usually started. Our lord and master disappears off to his private quarters and she uses the time to poke her nose into absolutely everything she can. The master comes out, sometimes days later, sometimes after a few hours. They throw more insults at each other. The mistress demands payment for the insults, he throws her a rock that's probably worth millions on the open market on earth, although I wouldn't know because I'm barely allowed...."

"Folsom," Hades warned. "You know full well why you're no longer allowed to go shopping on earth. Stick to the point."

"I'll tell you about it later," Folsom whispered to Ali who was listening avidly. "Anyhow, where were we? Oh, yes, the rock throwing incidents, and then the mistress screams off back to the gate. The gates are usually already open for her by the time she gets there. She orders a few more demons around before she leaves, the gate closes, and the whole realm gives a huge sigh of relief until next time."

"None of that sounds very pleasant for anyone," Ali said thoughtfully, tapping his chin with his finger. "Have you ever tried anything different for when she arrives, maybe, so that the whole visit can go more smoothly."

"We've tried every damn thing. Do you know how much disruption she causes every time she sets foot in the gates?" Hades jumped off his throne, striding over to the fire pit, staring at the flames.

Folsom nodded. "Our master has tried seduction, lavish banquets, gifts of gold and precious gems, talking to her, and reasoning with her. One time he even ordered in three of the handsomest male courtesans you'd ever hope to meet and put them in her bedchamber, hoping they would put her in a better mood. She ordered the heads cut off two of the maids when they made the mistake of offering them breakfast the next morning while she was still in bed with them."

"Surely, she must have some redeeming qualities. She is a goddess in her own right," Hades heard Ali say. He snorted. Persephone had a lot of followers in her day, and they hailed her as the goddess who guaranteed fertility in their fields, but when she was in the Underworld, she was a totally different person.

"Not really, no." Folsom shook his head. "There's a reason why she's called the 'dread Persephone' and why, up there on earth, no one mentions the name of the Queen of the Underworld. She really took what it meant, being a ruler in this realm to heart."

"You think it's a psychological thing? That simply by being in this realm she turned into a not-nice person?" Ali's unusual question was enough to make Hades turn around.

"Persephone was a spoiled young lady who was doted on by her mother her whole life and never allowed to date until I swept her away. No man or god was good enough for the daughter of Demeter," he said angrily. "Her behavior had nothing to do with being down here, or being abducted. What did shape her attitude was the way Zeus, and Helios bowed down to the wishes of my damn sister, insisting that Persephone be allowed to have her way, retaining her title as Queen of the Underworld, without having to live with me full time. A title I never gave her, but at the time didn't object to for reasons I've already explained. But when she sweeps in here like her shit doesn't stink, you'll see why no one who worshipped her ever mentioned her by name."

"Well, she's not the Queen of the Underworld, now, is she?" Ali wriggled off his cushion and came running over. Hades was happy to catch him. Having Ali in his arms had a magical way of making him feel better. "I do think, that when she comes, we should all make a point of being nice to her, because this situation is going to be difficult enough for her as it is. Losing her title because you're mated to me, is likely to put a kink in her skirt."

Persephone's skirt was the last thing Hades was worried about, but Ali hadn't finished.

"Personally, I think it would be exciting to go for a ride in your carriage, so we can take that when we go to the gates tomorrow. I'd also like to pet some puppies, and meet some of your demons who are in charge around here before she comes. Do you think we can do that?"

Hades struggled to make sense of Ali's wishes. His thought process wasn't helped when his wee chipmunk started pressing kisses along his jaw. "By puppies, were you referring to the hellhounds, by any chance?" He asked, tilting his neck up, because Ali had sensual lips that felt heavenly on his skin.

"Bah. Puppies, hellhounds. What's the difference?" Ali smiled, the sun came out in the dim dark hall of the Underworld, and Hades was blinded by the beauty of it.

/~/~/~/~/

Apparently, there was a huge difference between hellhounds and cute little puppies. Ali eyed the six mammoth dogs guarding the gate, quietly quaking in his boots. All the dogs stood bigger than he did, and he was on two legs while they had four. The drool escaping their massive jowls, and their bright red eyes didn't help reduce their menacing demeanor.

Hades was introducing him to the largest hound. "Ali, my sweet, this is Juno. He runs the hellhounds, although Madison, who's married to

Death's son Sebastian, is the actual alpha of the hellhound pack. I'll arrange a dinner when this Persephone business has been resolved, so you can meet them all. Juno, this is my true mate, Ali. He will rule by my side from now on and will be respected in all things."

Ali's eyes widened as first Juno, then the other five dogs all sort of bowed. Well, their front legs buckled, and all six snouts were leaving drool on the ground. *Our Master is blessed indeed.* Ali wanted to turn around to see who was talking, but he couldn't take his eyes off the dogs.

Yes, it is I. The hound kneeling before you. Ali caught Juno's eye.

"You're talking to me through my mind? How cool is that?" Ali looked up at his mate, and refrained from bouncing on his toes, because he didn't want to embarrass Hades. "Can all hellhounds do that? Do they do that to everyone?"

"No, only Juno has that power, and he only talks to a very select few special people on this realm," Hades said with the glimmer of a smile. "You might want to tell them to get up, because a dog's knees can't support their weight for very long."

"Oh, my gosh, yes. Get up, get up." Ali waved his hands upwards. "You don't have to bow to me. I'm Hades' mate, and he claimed me, which you can probably scent, but apart from that I'm no one special."

You are the living embodiment of all that our Master has searched for, and will be treated accordingly. T'will be death to any who dishonor you on this realm. The hounds all got to their feet again. Ali would swear Juno was smirking and he blushed.

"Thanks." *I think.* Ali got the impression the huge dog was being totally sincere. He just wasn't sure threats of death were necessary in the Underworld when most of the inhabitants were already dead. "So," he said brightly, desperate to change the subject, "these are the famous gates. Are they for keeping spirits in, or out?"

"In," Hades said. "Originally, all souls used to come to the Underworld regardless of whether they had lived a good life, or committed atrocious sins. They were judged in the hall over there," he pointed to a huge rugged stone structure that might have once been made of white marble. "That used to house three judges who determined where a soul would go; usually one of the fields, but occasionally someone was sent to Tartarus. But none of that has happened in over a thousand years."

"What happened?" Ali was still getting over the fact there was so much light in the Underworld. Everything he'd ever read, and okay that wasn't much, suggested it was a very dark and gloomy place. But standing at the gates with his mate, it was just like being out on a cloudy day although he couldn't see a sun anywhere.

"Heaven happened." Hades wrinkled his nose. "When Jesus came down to earth roughly two thousand years ago he told everyone that his father's house had many mansions and they were built for all those who had lived a blameless life. The idea took – people expected their souls to rise to the heavens if they'd been good all their lives. Only those weighed down by sins had souls too heavy to reach those pearly gates, so the spirits find my gates instead. The three judges gave up, sent me a letter and told me they were retiring because anyone's soul who ended up here, was clearly a bad person. Those souls came under my domain."

"I'd better make sure I do something especially evil then, so when I die, I can stay down here with you." Ali was inspecting the humungous gate. It looked as though it was cast iron, but there was like a forcefield around it that would give anyone the idea that it was impenetrable. That's if they could get past the hellhounds first. It took him a moment to realize Hades and even the hellhounds seemed to be laughing.

"Did I say something funny?" He turned to look at his mate who was genuinely laughing.

"You were talking about your death." Hades chuckled some more.

Ali tapped his foot on the hard ground. It wasn't concrete, but his boots made a satisfying tap on it. "I realize death is just a concept to guys like you, and with so many spirits around, you're all probably used to it. But don't you think your gallows humor is going a bit too far? It was my death I was talking about."

"Babe, I am truly sorry." Hades rubbed his hand over his mouth as if to rub away his grin. He came over, placing his hand on the tattoo he'd left on Ali's skin. "Do you know what this mark means?"

"Yes." Ali was very proud of his mark. He'd even asked Hades to whip up the bright pink sleeveless t-shirt for him, so people could see it before they left the throne room. "It shows everyone that I'm your mate and they'd better not think about giving me any grief about it. It's a claiming mark, and one I absolutely adore because it's far better than any old teeth marks my family dream of wearing. But it's not as though it gives me any special powers or anything."

Hades was silent, staring at him as though he was someone special. Ali found he could get used to being treated like that, although that little logical part of his brain reminded him Hades hadn't answered his question. "Your mark doesn't give me any special powers, does it?"

"I guess that depends on what you mean by special powers." Hades' eyes flicked up at the sky, then across to Juno before they settled back on Ali's face. "Most people assume that immortality is pretty special, and then there's the ability to command the hellhounds, translocate to other realms including earth, walk through the Underworld gates without an invitation, and on earth you'd probably have no trouble locating seams of gold or precious metals, because they're under my rule as well. Oh, and the ability to become invisible simply by thinking about it."

"Get out of here." Ali grabbed Hades' hand in case his mate took him literally and disappeared. "I'm honestly immortal? I can stay with you until the end of time?"

"From the time you were born, your thread has become part of the main fabric in the weave of life," Hades said, deadly serious. "When I asked you to spend eternity with me, I meant it."

"Oh, my gods, oh, my gods, I can't believe it." Leaping up, Ali hooked his arms around his mate's neck. "I was so worried, not enough to not claim you of course, because you're amazing, but I was terrified of what might happen when I died before you. I didn't want to ever leave you to your lonely existence again. This is the most amazing news ever."

"Most people given the opportunity to dig for gold and treasures couldn't wait to blink out of here and start looking." Hades was teasing, Ali could tell, but he was so damn happy he didn't bother to come up with a comeback of his own.

"I'm so happy, so truly happy. I swear, you might not be when you get sick of my mouth somedays, but I'm just so glad you won't ever be alone again." Kissing. Kissing was definitely called for in a situation like this and as Hades' kisses were hotter than the fires of Tartarus (Ali was so proud of himself for learning new things), he almost missed Juno's comment in his head.

And that is why, when one puts the Master's life and happiness before his own, the hounds of hell and all who live here will gladly give their lives for the new Consort. Hail Ali, Lord of the Underworld! The dogs all lifted their muzzles and howled.

Lord of the Underworld. It had a nice ring to it. Ali just hoped it didn't mean he'd be expected to wear black all the time. It really wasn't his color.

Chapter Ten

Nerves. At least, that's what Hades was attributing to the butterflies fluttering around in his stomach. He wasn't going to show it, but as he prepared his horses, ready to pull his giant gold carriage for the short trip to the gates, Hades could admit to himself he was nervous. A visit from Persephone was never a pleasant way to spend the day.

"Why don't I see any spirits floating or walking around?" Ali asked. Perched on a hay bale he was watching what Hades was doing closely. "The demon villages you took me to yesterday were fascinating – I'd never thought baby demons could look so cute with their little tails, horns and scales, but I haven't seen a single floaty substance. Is it just because I'm a shifter and aren't wired for seeing ghosts?"

"Ghosts and the souls we have here are two separate things, my sweet." Hades wasn't going to communicate any of his anxiety to his mate – not intentionally at least. He wasn't sure what their bond was doing because Ali preferred to use his mouth for communication, which Hades was enjoying more than he thought he would. "The ghosts humans speak of on the earth realm are disembodied spirits caught between living and the afterlife. They might not have accepted they are dead, or in most cases, the spirit has a strong attachment to someone or something where they died, and they refuse to move on. They are the floaty things you're referring to. Souls down here look as though they did when they were living."

"But doesn't your friend, Death take care of spirits who won't go where they're supposed to?"

Hades tightened the girth strap he was working on and stood up. Ali was a splash of color in the dark stables with his bright pink tank top and his white jeans. "Sweetheart, Death would be run off his feet if he had to attend every death as they occur, and his new mate wouldn't be happy with me if I insisted on that happening."

Stroking down Alastor's rump, Hades moved onto Nyctaeus who was moving his feet impatiently. "I know, I know, you don't get to go out nearly as often as you'd like to," he grinned as the horse tried to nip him. The four horses were almost identical in looks, and as young and fresh looking now as they were the day they came into being. But his famous immortal steeds had totally different personalities. "Thanatos only attends the passing of specific souls – ones that the Fates favor, or perhaps those that need comfort as they leave their body. Other souls are particularly heinous, and Thanatos has to literally drag them down here. But it's not possible for him to attend to everyone who dies."

Ali scrunched up his nose. "So, you don't actually have a say on who dies, or who goes where when they die?"

Hades shook his head. Nyctaeus took the opportunity to get his nip in this time, catching Hades on the top of his arm. Hades grinned and patted his fine stead's neck as he ran the bridle over his up-pricked ears. "No," he said, responding to his mate's question. "It is entirely up to the Fates who lives, who dies, and when. They communicate directly with Thanatos who goes where he's directed. Gods can kill people, any being really, and sometimes that's the Fates will that it happens that way. But, in these modern times, the Fates can get very nasty if someone breaks the life thread of an individual before their time. It can leave a hole in the tapestry of life."

"When I meet Thanatos, I'll be sure to ask him to pass on a message to the Fates thanking them for my wonderful mate," Ali said cheerily. "But you still haven't explained where all the souls down here are. I thought this place would be full of them."

"It is. I just don't need to see them by the house." Hades tightened the last buckle and grabbed the reins dangling from his four horses before climbing onto the seat. "Come on, babe, climb up and I'll explain as we head to the gates. It won't help Persephone's mood if she's kept waiting."

"She's a goddess," Ali said, scampering over and climbing up next to Hades. "I'm sure she'll be nice once she's faced with my sunny personality."

Hades managed not to snort. Orphnaeus did it for him. Clicking his tongue against the roof of his mouth, Hades signaled his horses to move. Ali jolted and squealed as they took off. "This is so exciting," he yelled, clinging onto Hades' arm. "I feel like someone super important in this carriage."

"You are," Hades yelled back as he juggled his reins to let the horses have their head. He really should have taken them out more often. They thundered along the carriage way, manes flying and hooves pounding the asphalt. Because of their speed, they would make the trip to the Gates in no time. Unwilling to be early for their appointment, Hades guided them around one of the tracks that overlooked the fields. Demons dove out of their way as the horses thundered on.

As they moved further away from the mansion, the first of many hut villages appeared. Easing the reins back slowly, Hades urged his horses into a gentle clop. "These are where some of the less evil souls live," he said pointing to where a large group of men were attempting to break huge black rocks with tiny chisels. "I have over a thousand quarries where souls like this work six days a week for twelve hours a day."

"They're not screaming." Ali stood up so he could see over the edge of the carriage. "What did they do in life that had them sent here?"

"They're corporate souls, most of them, and they work too hard to even think about screaming." Hades scanned the crowd waiting for one to catch his eye. "You there. Come here," he ordered when one finally glanced his way.

The man looked at his friends, and then up at a tall black demon who was supervising. He waited until he got the nod before running over.

"My Lord," he said, falling to his knees beside the carriage, his forehead kissing the ground. "Such an honor to be noticed. How might I serve you today, oh high lord, that I might commute my sentence and be moved to more favorable quarters."

Ignoring the man for the moment, Hades looked at his mate. "This guy clearly hasn't been here very long. He's still carrying the overly large sense of entitlement he had that put him down here in the first place. He should know better than to expect favors from me."

"Can they work their way to a better position?" Ali asked. "If they are good long enough that is. How long is a sentence for men like this?"

"There's a sliding scale depending on an individual's crime." Hades looked down his nose at the man still prostrate on the ground. "You there. What crime were you charged with and how old were you when you died?"

"I didn't do much at all, mighty Lord," the man protested as he sat up. "It really wasn't my fault. The investors...."

"What crime?" Hades snapped. Someone should've told the idiot in front of him that the 'wasn't my fault' excuse was guaranteed to piss him off. Souls were judged, the weight on their soul proof enough of any wrongdoing. Mouthing off and trying to shift the blame elsewhere didn't help any soul's cause.

"I was CEO of one of the biggest investment companies in Europe. I gave hundreds of people jobs, looked after billions of dollars for a huge range of private investors." The man wore a proud look even though he was still on his knees.

"The crime." Hades wasn't interested in a resume.

"I was doing a lot of good in the community," the man protested.

"Braxel," Hades called out to the demon supervisor. "What was this soul's crime? I'm trying to give an example to my mate about sentencing, and this guy keeps waffling on about shit I don't care about."

"My lord, Lord Consort," the demon came over, pulling a notebook from his pocket. "Number 692. Avarice." He glanced at the man. "Yep, that's him. Embezzled four point two billion dollars which was made up of the life savings of twenty two thousand, four hundred and ninety six mom and pop investors causing years of havoc for them. Also found guilty of underpaying four hundred and sixty four workers who were living in slum conditions. Pride. Envy, and Sloth are also mentioned, not to mention numerous counts of adultery. Age at death, seventy three earth years. Died from a combination of Lust and Gluttony."

"Thank you Braxel." Hades waved for the demon to continue his work and turned to Ali. "So, you see, sweet one, in this situation we have multiple sins, with a base age of seventy three years. Now, normally plain investment fraud resulting in the pain of others, which is so damn common you would not believe, that would result in a soul being punished for seven times his natural lifetime which in this case would be five hundred and eleven years. However, because his soul also holds the weight of five other major sins, his punishment lifetime is multiplied by five – five sins, five times the lifetime count – meaning this individual will be breaking rocks six days a week, for two thousand, five hundred and fifty five years."

Ali's face seemed to pale, but then his sweet mate shook himself and plastered a wide grin on his sweet face. "I guess that's not so bad when you consider he's down here for eternity. What will happen to him once he's served his sentence here? Does he get to live a normal life down here then?"

"It doesn't work like that, sweetness," Hades shook his head. "Each sin carries a different punishment, so when he's finished doing this work to repay the debt on his soul, he'll be given a different punishment relating to one of his other sins for the two thousand odd years he owes, and then the next one and so on. Folsom has a flow chart I'm sure he'd be thrilled to show you when we get back."

"Can't they ever redeem themselves, ever?" Ali asked, and Hades noted the catch in his mate's throat. The damned soul was crying, as if that would make any difference.

Picking up the reins again, Hades urged his horses into a trot. "There have been instances," he said as the carriage started to move, "of a soul doing a completely selfless, heroic act, that automatically wipes the weight of his sins from his soul. Unfortunately, it is very rare for that to happen."

"But when it does?" Ali was clutching his arm again and Hades felt the warmth of them spread through his body. "Is it like in the movies? Does the soul suddenly become bathed in a white light, and they're lifted up and taken to heaven or one of the heavenly fields, to live a life in comfort and peace?"

"You've got it exactly right," Hades smiled at his hopeful mate. "An ascension is a time for celebration down here. It gives the other souls hope that they too can be lifted if they think of others and act on those thoughts." He didn't mention that the last time they had an ascension was more than a hundred years before.

Noting the gates coming up, and the white flash behind it, he gnawed the inside of his lip. "Babe, you know...."

"Don't take anything your ex Queen says to me personally. Remember that I have as much standing in this world as you do, and she doesn't. I also know, because you've told me a dozen times, that this visit is temporary, and if all else fails bite my tongue until she's gone. You drilled all of this into me last night while you were plundering my body."

Fun times. Hades would have said more, but the carriage had arrived at the gates. Letting out a long breath,

Hades jumped down from his seat and hurried around the carriage to help Ali down. *If she fucks up my mating, I'll find a way to punish her for all eternity,* he thought. With a swirl of his coat and his mate tucked under his arm, Hades strode towards the gate.

Chapter Eleven

Ali was sure his eyes were going to fall out of his head. His rational brain knew that anyone who could be deemed a goddess was going to be beautiful, but seeing the evidence in the flesh was twenty thousand times more than he imagined.

Through the gates he could see the figure of a woman a lot taller than he was. Her blond hair was a mass of waves and curls all falling around her head like a stunning waterfall. Pale green eyes stared out from a classically beautiful face that hosted high cheek bones and full lush pale pink lips. In a word, Persephone was stunning. Ali could understand in a heartbeat why Hades had been so taken with her.

But none of Hades apparent lust or love showed on his face as he bid the gates to open. The six hellhounds from the day before all growled and slunk away as she walked through. Not sure his eyes could take the strain, Ali watched in disbelief as Persephone's full lips turned up in a snarl the moment the gates closed behind her.

"What magic is this?" She was truly snarling! Twirling around, her bright white gown flowed around her slender form. "Why haven't I changed in accordance to my position as queen? My robes and hair should be black, not white and gold. My feet should be clad in boots, not these skimpy sandals. My crown," she felt her hair. "What happened to my crown?"

"Clearly, my realm recognizes my new true mate as my co-ruler here, Persephone. I am just as surprised as you are, although heartily pleased the realm reacted so quickly. The Underworld has no need for a Queen anymore, and the fact you retained your look as Goddess of the fields reflects that," Hades said shortly. His lips curled up slightly at the edges. "The dread Persephone is no more. My eternity of torment for the sake of one thoughtless act is finally over."

"That's not possible." Hands fisted at her sides, Persephone howled. "Being queen is my right, bestowed on me by Zeus himself in repayment for your abduction of me and having to suffer your unruly lusts."

"You never once suffered from my lusts, as you well know and remind me of frequently," Hades said coolly. "The one mistake I ever made was abducting you in front of witnesses, but that was a million moons ago and ever since that day, myself and this realm have suffered from your manic drive for power. From this point onwards, you no longer have any jurisdiction here, so state your business and be gone."

"Oh, so that's your little game is it?" Persephone sneered as she stalked closer. "You've finally gotten so frustrated at having nothing but your hand around that worthless cock of yours, you've used your powers to make me think I've been stripped of my title, just so I'll sleep with you to get my rights back. You must think I'm stupid, but I see through your little games."

"Hades' cock is not worthless, and he's not playing games," Ali said, shaking off his awe at seeing a real live goddess and jumping feet first into the conversation. "Hades is a good, kind, and attentive lover, who knows how to make my body sing and when he shoves his cock up my ass, I feel possessed, cherished and loved for all eternity. Just because you've lost your chance at my hunky man, you've got no call to slander him. Don't ever let me hear you run down my mate like that again."

"Who the hell are you?" Persephone waved her hand, finally noticing him for the first time and not in a good way. "Bow down before me, pissant, before I sew your mouth up for speaking to me in that way. Bow down, I order you. Get on your knees."

Ali felt a small tug, like a compulsion almost, but it was just as quickly gone. "I'm not bowing to you. You might be a goddess, but your attitude needs a lot to be desired. I give my respect to people that have earned it and you definitely haven't. You come in here where you're not welcome, upsetting Hades and the hellhounds and I notice none of the demon guards that were here yesterday are here today. You have a nasty attitude lady."

"Hades." Persephone's voice was like thunder as she continued to wave her arms in Ali's direction. "You may have stripped my powers in this realm. I don't know how, and I demand them back, but make this insect kneel before me at once. I demand it."

"You don't have the right to demand anything on this realm anymore, Persephone," Hades' quiet voice was a contrast to the goddess's yelling. "The realm has acknowledged Ali's right as my mate to rule this realm by my side. Which means none of your powers will ever work against him, on this realm or any other. They didn't work on me; they won't work on him."

"She tried to use her powers against you?" Ali was horrified as he stared up at his mate. "Did she hurt you, are you okay?" He turned back to Persephone who was eying him with disgust. "How could you do that? You're supposed to be a nice person. Centuries ago, thousands of people worshipped you, so you'd keep their fields safe and give them good harvests. Using your powers on a god who let you be queen for eons is just not a nice thing to do."

"Are you deliberately trying to tell me how to behave?" Persephone's voice rose to screaming pitch. "You dare to stand before a goddess and criticize my behavior?"

"Someone has to," Ali said just as hotly. "You made Hades feel bad when he abducted you, and brought you down here. You treated him like shit and made him feel like he wasn't good enough no matter what he did. If you spent five minutes getting to know him, you'd know what a kind and decent guy he truly is, but you didn't bother, did you?"

"You do know what Hades does for a living, don't you?" Persephone seemed genuinely incredulous. "He tortures people for eternity!"

No wonder my poor mate is so misunderstood if his own Queen can't be supportive. "My mate keeps the evil souls from wandering the earth and protects the living. He provides the punishments designed to help those souls learn the wrongness of their horrible deeds on earth. Hades was given a job to do and he's done it without complaint since he lost the coin toss he had with his brothers. He's doing his job, and he does it really well. What's your excuse?"

"I don't know what you're talking about."

Persephone might seem like she didn't know what he was referring to, but Ali wasn't fooled especially when she kept glancing at Hades as though she wanted to jump him. *Not on my watch,* he thought fiercely. "I'm talking about you, with your attitude. I've only been down here a day and not one person, demon, or spirit here has a nice thing to say about you. They all recognize Hades as a fair and just god who has to do a shitty job, but what about you? You've done nothing but stamp your foot and yell since you got here. I thought goddesses were supposed to be the nice guys."

"I am nice." Persephone drew herself up proudly, running her hands down her torso deliberately. "My reputation as a great beauty precedes me. Men from all realms have craved for just one of my smiles. Hades especially. If I clicked my fingers, Hades would be on his knees, kissing my feet."

"No, I wouldn't."

"No, he wouldn't," Ali repeated his mate's fierce tone. "And don't go using your beauty like a tool. You'll set the women's movement back a hundred years with stupid ploys like that. You're classically beautiful – so what? If you haven't got the brains and sweet personality to match, then you're nothing but a pretty ornament. Hades deserves better than you and he always has."

Ali was fairly sure no one had ever spoken to the goddess in that tone before. She tilted her head, eyeing him like a specimen in a jar. "Who are you again, and what business do you have, being in the Underworld?"

"I am Ali, Hades' mate, and Lord of the Underworld in my own right," Ali said proudly, wishing he was taller as he straightened his back. "The hellhounds listen when I call, the demons respond to my requests, but more importantly, because Hades is my mate, I will defend him, his honor, and this realm to the death if necessary."

Sliding his arm around Hades' waist, the man was standing like a statue, Ali widened his smile as he felt his mate lean into him slightly.

Persephone edged a little closer, wrinkling her nose. "You're nothing but a chipmunk shifter – a living one at that. How on earth did you get down here? There's no way the miserly lord of the Underworld would've met you anywhere else than here. The living do not belong here. How did you find a way to bypass the gates and rigid rules this place is bound by? If you've snuck in here, mate claim or not, it's the death penalty for you and Hades will have no choice but to uphold the sentence."

"We met at a wedding, mutual friends of ours." Ali smiled up at his stoic mate. "It was so heroic. He saved me, you know, from an overzealous wolf shifter. He picked me up and held me in his arms, brought me to our new home and marked me for eternity. It's amazing, you should see what I've done to the place. Honestly, all that black was so drab but now the living areas are filled with color. My mate is so good to me."

"It's easy to give you what you ask for, because you're so good to me," Hades said softly. Ali could see the warmth in his eyes, but those same eyes hardened again when Hades looked at Persephone. "Your time here is done, Persephone. I had nothing to do with stripping you of your title, your crown, or anything else. This realm is a living entity in its own right and it decided who would rule here. I'm glad it's done, though, as it saved me from doing it. My wonderful Ali now rules by my side and will forever more. You have no reason to ever see my ugly face again, or spend time in the realm you've done nothing but complain about. The demons, Furies, Hellhounds and souls who reside here will no longer heed your call, or respond to your orders. The reign of the dread queen Persephone is finally over. I have a true and decent Lord to rule by my side forever more."

"You're gay?"

Ali tutted as he shook his head. "Didn't you hear anything my mate just said? Why do you care how Hades identifies himself, or who he sleeps with? You never wanted him like I do, so just forget about it. Go rule your fields or whatever else it is you do when you're not upsetting my mate. Isn't it great? You don't have to come down here anymore. That must be so liberating for you."

Persephone's mouth opened and closed like a fish. "I'm queen in this realm," she said finally. "I'm the dread queen Persephone, co-ruler of the Underworld."

"Not any more you aren't. Get with the program." Sighing, Ali slipped away from Hades' side and took the goddesses arm, leading her back towards the gate. "Don't take it badly," he said as kindly as he could. He was still upset at Persephone maligning a cock she hadn't even seen.

"You never liked it down here anyway," he continued. "The sun never shines, and everyone spends all their time screaming and complaining. You clearly didn't like the mansion, or you'd have redecorated eons ago, and Hades explained how you never wanted to sleep with him, or even give him a smile, so you clearly don't like him either. Let's just end things amicably, okay? You go your way and leave us to muddle along without you. You'll see it's the best for all of us. Open," he called to the gates which swung open silently.

"There you go," Ali said, letting go of Persephone's arm and giving her a tiny push. "You go do your goddess things and leave us to have fun down here. Bye now. Don't bother to write. Shut," he added as soon as Persephone stumbled over the line between the Underworld and the nothing beyond it. The gates clanged as they swiftly shut firmly, and Ali waved as Persephone just stood there on the other side. "Hades and I are going to have a carriage ride now, and then we're going home for a wonderful lunch and an afternoon sexy romp. Have a nice eternity. Bye."

He turned around to see Hades standing with open arms. "Yee ha," he yelled as he ran across the asphalt and into his mate's arms. Hades swung him around and then kissed him soundly.

When Ali could finally come up for air, he blinked up at his mate who had a smile a mile wide. "Not that I'm complaining, but what was that for?"

"You know exactly what you did," Hades said fondly, tapping him lightly on the nose with his finger. "Did I hear you mention a carriage ride? My horses are going to love you as much as the hellhounds do."

"Yep," Ali said happily. "I'm sure I've still got a lot more to see. Show me your world, oh great Lord. The carriage gives me an excuse to snuggle with you while we talk. I'm going to become addicted to it, I can tell."

Hades didn't seem to mind, or if he did, it didn't show in the hot kiss that followed, or the one after that.

Chapter Twelve

Love. For Hades it had always been nothing more than a concept, written about by poets, used as an excuse for war, and something definitely alien to his life. But as he wielded his reins, urging his horses to take them around his domain, he had to wonder if he had finally found a person whom he could love. Totally. Unreservedly. For all time. A special someone who would love him in return.

It was a scary concept. As one who'd been shunned by others his entire life, with the exception of his brothers, Hades could hardly dare hope that special person was now sitting by his side. Oh, he knew the stories of Fated Mates. He'd seen for himself how love had turned his brother Poseidon from a man with a revolving bedroom door, into the most devoted and faithful of partners. Sei had said he would give up the sea for his mate. Hades didn't have that option.

Hades wanted to believe, he truly did. He'd spent years wandering the earth hoping to feel that spark, see the light, find his person. Ali had jumped into his hands, and into his heart, but a small part of Hades still held back. Even after Ali's staunch defense of him with Persephone, one thing his former queen said still rang true. Hades did torture people – or rather he devised the tortures for those beings whose crimes were either against the gods, or so horrific on earth a tedious and never ending rock cutting job wasn't punishment enough.

He had no choice but to share that part of himself with Ali. It was only fair. Tugging the reins, Hades encouraged the horses to move towards what was laughingly known among the demons as the "pain pits." If he was going to give his heart fully to the sweet soul he was bound to, then Ali had to know the true horror of where he lived and who Hades truly was. Know it and accept it.

"Where I'm taking you now is not pleasant," Hades warned Ali as the faint sound of screams got steadily louder over the pounding of the horses' hooves. "There are so many different sins, and they are all punished in unique ways. What you saw earlier at the quarry were men who'd gained incredible wealth from the labors of others, hurting those others in the process. Their punishment is endless frustrating hard work. There are other souls who are driven by unnatural lust who are forced to participate in an endless orgy where they can never find their release. Pedophiles and people who commit crimes against children are usually dealt with by the Furies and all you need to know about that is they live up to their name. Many of the punishments are painful – all of them are frustratingly endless. Those who've committed crimes on the horrific end of the scale will never achieve ascension."

He hesitated. Ali looked up at him so trustingly and Hades hated that he was going to wipe that trust off his mate's sweet face. "I need to show you." He swallowed hard. "Persephone wasn't wrong when she said that I torture people, and while I am so proud of how quickly you defended me, you need to see and know the worst for yourself. After today, you need never visit this part of the realm again, but this is part of who I am and what I do. Part of what you rule over too."

Forcing his eyes back on the road, Hades was surprised by Ali's response. "I'm probably going to need ear plugs," Ali said as they got closer to the screaming. "I have really sensitive ears, you see. Being a shifter and all that."

"You can have ear plugs. You can have anything you like," Hades said quickly. "I'd do anything to spare you this, but...."

"You want me to see the worst of you and this realm," Ali said easily. "I get it. I do. There's a part of you that's worried I'm going to leave you, or worse, shun you like Persephone did and yet we'd have to stay together because of our bond. Believe me, you haven't seen torture until you've been forced to sit through a dinner with my family."

"You have issues with your family?" Hades knew for a fact nothing on earth came close to the eternal torment possible in Tartarus, or the pits that surrounded it. Ali would learn that for himself soon enough.

"They never forgave me for saving Claude's life and staying to be a friend to him afterwards. I have a very snobby and elitist family." Ali wiped the sweat from his brow. "It's a lot hotter here than at the mansion."

"Eternal heat is part of the torment. The fire pit in my office leads directly to the heart of Tartarus. You saved Claude's life – Sei's Claude, my brother in law?"

"Meh, it's a boring story," Ali waved it off. "It was more a case of good luck rather than strategy, but Claude's a friendly guy, and my family never approved of me, even before that happened. After I got shunned by the scurry, I moved to Tulsa on Claude's invite, and hadn't left. It was decades ago, back in the nineteen twenties, but my family can hold a grudge forever."

"I can't believe you're over a hundred years old." Hades took a double look at his mate. If he had to guess, he'd say Ali was no more than twenty five.

"Shifter genetics, mate of mine," Ali grinned. "Besides, you're one to talk. You don't look a day over thirty and I know you've been around since the dawn of time."

"Not quite, but close," Hades agreed. Age was just a number. For gods and paranormals, many of them didn't show a change in age after thirty. Once a paranormal was officially an adult, usually around twenty one to twenty five years of age, the concept of how old they were didn't matter. Definitely not between mates. "You're going to tell me about the saving of Claude, and your family one day when you trust me, but for now, we'd better stop for a moment so you can put in some ear plugs. The pits are just over there." He pointed to the twenty foot high wall denoting his maximum security area.

Pulling his horses to a stop, Hades held out his hand. The ear plugs in his palm were specifically designed to fit snugly into Ali's ears. Ali took them, but as he went to put them in, Hades held his hand. "You must harden your heart," he warned. "No matter what you see or hear, you must trust me that every soul that is kept behind those walls, have deserved their fate. Some of the people you'll see have been here for almost as long as this place has existed. In many of those cases I wasn't responsible for putting those beings here. Other gods cursed those souls for whatever reasons, and those people will never be released. In the last thousand years or so, it's been my responsibility and only the blackest of souls were condemned in the pits, purely because their crimes against others were so heinous, they could never be redeemed. Please, ask any questions of me, but don't speak to the souls directly. Not until you know their story. Is that okay?"

"They're criminals, right?"

Hades nodded. "They've all broken serious laws relating to their time period and customs."

"And I'm not going to find people behind those walls who've broken some silly law, like had anal sex with someone? Because in some countries that's still illegal. Or like, in Japan, it can be illegal to be fat in some companies. Or, or, how you aren't allowed to wear lacy underpants in Russia because they don't have enough cotton in them, or like having sex before marriage in Georgia, Idaho or Virginia, because that's illegal there too."

Hades had to grin. Only his mate would know trivial details like that. "We only condemn those who break serious universal laws," he said. "Multiple murders, crimes against innocents, malicious dictators, people like that."

Ali inhaled sharply. "Okay, lets do this. The sooner you show me the wretched underbelly of your realm, the sooner we can go home, have lunch and enjoy some snuggle time in that huge bed of yours."

"Our bed." Letting go of Ali's hands, Hades picked up the reins again. There was no way Ali was walking anywhere in the pits. Hades trusted his horses to move faster than any being contained in the hell of his domain. The urge to just dash them through rode him high, but Hades knew Ali needed time to absorb all he would see. Encouraging his horses to move swiftly, Hades headed for the wall. Ali's scream was added to the others as the horses and carriage went straight through what appeared to be a solid concrete wall.

/~/~/~/~/

"You didn't tell this carriage could go through bricks!" Ali thumped his mate on the arm as he tried to catch his breath. Seeing that ginormous wall come closer and closer, the horses' hooves pounding, manes and tails flying, and the carriage showing no sign of stopping damn near gave him a heart attack.

Hades muttered something, but thanks to the ear plugs, Ali couldn't hear him and whatever Hades had to say, it couldn't compete with Ali's sudden attack of nausea. Spread out before him was what he always imagined the Christian version of hell would be like and it was not pleasant.

The heat hit him first. Unmerciful, it covered Ali like a thick blanket, as though he'd just walked into a giant furnace someone had turned on high. Most of the souls he could see, and even the demon guards, were wearing little more than a thong – some of them didn't even bother with that. Ali wasn't sure what was worse – the naked dirty skin on show, or the demon guards lack of modesty.

But worse than the heat was the stench. Ali considered the smell of burnt flesh, blood, and decay a form of torture on its own and that's without the physical punishments he was witnessing.

They're already dead, he reminded himself crossly, as his heart winced, and he was ready to defend a man lashed to a whipping post. *They deserve all this,* he rationalized as he watched a man getting his whole body crushed by a boulder. The soul was strapped to what looked like train tracks, the boulder suspended high above him by a chain thicker than Ali's arm. He held his breath, watching as the boulder went up and up, hovered for a moment and then came crashing down again. Ali turned his head as the boulder started to lift up again.

Desperate souls scrabbled, trying to climb super shiny walls that offered them no grip and no chance of escape. Demons stood around watching the pitiful efforts, laughing as the souls thudded to the ground again. There were countless more in huge black iron cages, bound like animals – some of them feral. And through it all was the incessant screaming. How anyone could think with all the noise and commotion was beyond Ali's comprehension. His soul ached at the suffering and hate in the air. Everywhere he looked Ali saw men pushed to acts of desperation, their bodies broken under their relentless punishments, but of course there was no reprieve.

I know Hades believes this is necessary, but I do wish those horses could go just a little bit faster. Ali got it, he truly did. After meeting Persephone, it was only natural Hades was going to think his mate couldn't handle the nastier aspects of his job either. There was no telling how much damage that woman had done to Hades' psyche over the centuries. Ali would handle it – he would make himself cope with any of the sights he could never unsee. He kept telling himself that, chanting the words in his head, but even Ali could feel the tightness of his jaw, and the way his eyes were drawn to the horror that surrounded him.

The horses slowed. *Oh my gods, no, I thought we were getting out of here,* but as Ali looked over Hades' arms, his breath was sucked away as he spied a truly beautiful man, sitting on what appeared to be a beach chair, wearing a sack for a shirt and reading a magazine. He stood out, not only because of his inhuman beauty, but because he was the only person who was clean. Ali was still wondering how that was even possible considering even the horses' legs were coated in dust, when Hades pulled the carriage to a stop.

Chapter Thirteen

"Baby?" The last person Hades expected to see was his nephew. "What the hell are you doing in my pits?"

"Hey Uncle, nice chipmunk you've got there. Is this a new fetish kink of yours, driving your potential bedmates around your domain so you can scare the pants off them instead of undoing a zipper like the rest of us manage to do?" Baby looked up, flicking his hair off his face. Hades hadn't seen his nephew for a while, but even he could see Baby's stressed expression.

"Show some respect." Hades jumped down from the carriage and held out a hand for Ali who climbed down after him. "This is Ali, my mate. We met yesterday. I'm showing him around."

"Another mate? The Fates have been busy." Baby flicked a page of his magazine. "Nice to meet you, Ali. I think I remember seeing you at Sei's wedding. Don't go telling my dads I'm here, there's a good chap."

"What have you done now?" Hades huffed. Circling his hand in the air, he created a cone of silence around the three of them, so his mate could take out his ear plugs. "You're welcome in my domain, of course, but why the pits? Why didn't you come up to the house if you wanted to see me?"

"I didn't think you were here." Baby shrugged. "Artie said you were busy mate hunting. But then, you've found him, so I guess there's no need to go roaming the earth like a lost soul anymore."

Hades bit back his initial angry response. He was never lost, just always searching. He wasn't close to Baby, but only a tormented soul would feel at home in the pits and he felt compelled to ask. "Baby, what's wrong?"

"Er, excuse me." Ali tapped his shoulder, grabbing Hades' attention. "Not wanting to sound like a jealous shrew or anything similar, but why are you calling this dreamy looking guy Baby in front of me? I didn't expect that from you, Mate."

"Oh, Ali, I'm sorry." Hades tugged him close and tucked his irate mate under his arm. "I call him Baby, because that's what his family call him. I don't think he has another name. This is my nephew, Poseidon's son to Himeros, god of desire. The sack cloth is a new look though."

"Sorry," Ali scuffed his boot in the dust. "I haven't got used to the family dynamics yet." He looked around and Hades felt a tremble run through his mate's slender body. "Weird place for sunbathing if you don't mind me saying."

"Oh hey, I get it," Baby said breezily. "This place is the pits, literally, but it was the only place I could think of where I couldn't do any damage."

"Damage?" Leaving Ali for a moment, Hades knelt by his nephew's chair. "Baby, what's happening? What's going on with you? You didn't look your normal flirty self at your father's wedding, and this is the last place I expected to find you."

Baby sniffed and shrugged. He didn't seem to want to meet Hades' eyes.

"Didn't want to give the old man any trouble, did I. He's looked for eons to find someone to commit his battered heart to who'd actually look after it. I wasn't going to wreck his day."

"Wreck it how?" Ali asked. Hades felt his presence behind his back. "You don't seem the type to cause any trouble for anyone."

"I can't help it, can I?" Baby was shrugging so often Hades was starting to wonder if he had a shoulder affliction. "Trouble follows me. I make some random comment or give someone the eye – man or woman it doesn't seem to make any difference – and suddenly there's a fight, or a freaking riot. I don't cause it. I never start anything intentionally. It's not as though I can help the way I am. It just sucks that's all. I wish just once I could have someone non-family who could give me a hug and want to be with me without all the drama."

"Baby." Hades ran his hand through his hair in frustration. "You're right, you can't help who you are, but sunbathing in the pits is a step too far. It's not as though this realm even sees the sun."

"I like this place. It's not like I need an invite to visit this part of the realm." Baby smiled and it was as if he glowed. *No wonder the kid gets into so much trouble.* "Face it, no one's got the energy or the drive to try and get into my pants down here. Your demons are too cowed by you to try anything with me. It's one of the few places I can be left alone."

Ali's hand gripped Hades' shoulder. "You could come up to the house," he offered. Ali was so sweet and accepting. It was Hades' turn to glow this time with pride. "There's barely anyone there. The chairs are more comfortable, and there's plenty of food. Hades showed me an awesome library earlier. There's even a pool."

"A pool?" Baby's smile got wider, and Hades felt slightly embarrassed. "That wasn't there the last time I visited."

"I have a mate now. The place needed a few modifications." Hades stood up, catching his mate under his arm. "You're welcome, Baby. I know we don't chat much, but if you're looking for some peace and time on your phone, the house is a lot quieter than here."

Ali wrinkled his nose. "Smells better too."

Baby leapt to his feet and executed a courtly bow. "I've never felt more welcome," he said straightening up. "I can tell you don't expect anything from me, and you're not going to hassle me like...." He snapped his mouth shut but recovered quickly. "I'll take you up on it. You won't know that I'm there, although I could give your sex energies a bit of a boost if you're having any trouble in that direction, Uncle? After all, I imagine it's been a while." He actually had the audacity to wink.

"Hades doesn't need any help in that department," Ali said hotly. "Thank you for your offer, weird though it was. But you are welcome. You're welcome here and at the house in Greece, isn't he, Hades?"

Hades winced, then hoped Baby didn't notice.

"Too many people there, Uncle Ali," Baby said quickly. "Honestly, this realm is fine for a while. I promise I won't get in your way. It's enough that no one can find me here."

Hmm. Hades nodded. "We're busy the rest of the afternoon, but you can join us for dinner about eight if you're hungry. In the meantime, we have places to be. Pop your ear plugs in, sweetness. I'll get you out of here before those cute eardrums of yours burst."

"Cute eardrums? That's positively adorable," Baby beamed. "I didn't know you had it in you, Uncle, but I'm so glad you do. Lovely to meet you, Uncle Ali. I'll see you at dinner."

It really is hot here, and that was the reason Hades was giving for his overly heated cheeks and he'd smite anyone who thought it might be otherwise.

But as he urged the horses to take the carriage out of the pits, that insidious voice inside his head was whispering, *Ali's too good for you, he's too damn good for the likes of you. Standing up to Persephone for you, accepting Baby and the horror of the Pits. You don't deserve a man like that. You don't deserve any sweetness in your life. You know what you do. You know who you are. You should let him go before you wreck his soul like everyone else you come into contact with.*

What was worse? Hades knew his inner voice was right.

/~/~/~/~/

"Do your family visit a lot?" Ali asked, lying back in Hades' arms, watching the sea of flowers below them. Neither one of them had said much at all as they'd exited the pits. Ali handled being driven through a wall a bit easier the second time around. The silence between them continued during the rest of the drive, even when Hades pulled up on a giant cliff, which offered a beautiful view of the lush fields below. Ali suspected he was looking at the Elysium fields where heroes and warriors of old spent their eternity. But he didn't want to talk about the diverse realm anymore – he wanted to know more about his mate.

"Huh?" Hades shook his head. As Ali suspected, his mate seemed deep in thought. "The family? No. My brothers use orbs if they want to speak to me, which isn't often. I have very little to do with my sisters. I bump into my nephews occasionally when I'm on earth, like if one of them is at Claude's for example. That was only a recent thing. My family aren't close, especially with me."

That's so damn sad. "Well, you have me now," Ali said brightly, determined to find a way to bolster Hades' mood. "Enough about stupid family members who don't know what they're missing. Did I pass the test? I didn't scream when we visited the pits. Well," he amended, "only a little bit, but I didn't expect you to drive me through a solid wall. I didn't throw up, although that was also a possibility because it really stinks in there. But can't you see? There's nothing you can do or show me that's going to make me turn away from you."

Hades was silent for so long, Ali's stomach started to churn, and his chipmunk chattered loudly in his head. The view was beautiful, and Hades' chest was still solid against his back, but Ali could feel the gulf between them getting wider and wider – in his head at least.

Which meant he couldn't keep his mouth shut. "Oh, I see your problem," he said far louder than he meant to. "Now you think I'm some sort of sick puppy because I didn't get revolted by what I saw. You expected me to scream, or faint, or throw up and demand to be taken out of that wretched place and because I didn't do that, you think there's something wrong with me. Or worse, you think I'm going to become immune to all the pain around here. What do you think I'm going to do? Insist on dressing all in black, not bloody likely, and prance about with a crown on my head? Are you worried I've become the dread Ali now?"

Swiveling around on Hades' lap, Ali put his hands on his hips and gave his mate his fiercest scowl. "You don't get to judge me, Mister. I don't judge you and never would. I'm prepared to support everything about you, so the least you can do is give me the same damn respect. I'm not going to lie. It's impossible for me to lie to you and yes, if you really want to know, I hated that horrible place. Any halfway decent person would shudder and recoil at seeing such depravity and suffering. But I trust you. You told me before we even went in there that every single person in the pits deserved to be there. So that's it. I accepted it. But you don't get to give me the cold shoulder now just because I'm good at hiding how freaking horrified I was by that place."

Hades' face was a mask. Not a muscle twitched, and for some reason that indifference sent Ali's emotions rocketing. "The pits aren't you," he said urgently, his heart hammering. "They are part of your realm, just like those beautiful flowers down there." He flung out an arm for emphasis. If Hades didn't say something soon, he'd be pacing along the cliff edge, or throwing himself off it.

"There seems to be so many facets of the Underworld. Believe me, I'm knock me over with a feather surprised. Before coming here, my imagination had me thinking the Underworld was all heat, fire, and the screams of the damned, but the diversity down here's incredible. You've shown me so much and it's only been one day. I want to spend a thousand lifetimes learning so much more about this realm and *you*." Ali prodded Hades' chest with his finger for emphasis.

"You're the important thing here. Didn't you kiss my lips off when I stood up for you with your ex? Say something damn it. Even if it's just to tell me to rack off, say something!"

"You shine." Hades shook his head although his expression didn't change. "Your inner light is brighter than any sun I've seen."

There's more than one sun? "Is that a problem for you? Do you need to wear sunglasses around me or something? Do you only notice that here, or is it everywhere we go?"

Hades shook his head again. *Use your words, damn it.* "It's not that. You… you…. How can you be so accepting of all this?"

There was so much passion behind those simple words, Ali was shocked, especially when Hades' facial expression didn't change. But Ali rallied quickly. "I can accept any of this because I care about you, dim wit. Those biddies upstairs, or wherever they are, gave me the most handsome, hunky, amazing man I have ever met to be mine to cherish forever. You think I'm going to reject a gift like that? You think I'm going to reject you?"

"You should." Hades turned his head. Ali wanted to grab the man by his chiseled cheeks and either slap him or kiss him senseless. "I'm not good for you. Spending an eternity down here would dull the brightest soul. You'd never have seen this wretched place, if it wasn't for me."

"Fuck that bitch and your family did a number on you." Ali winced as he realized he'd said that out loud. Grabbing Hades' shoulders, he shook him. "I could list a hundred ways I'm not good for you either," he said fiercely. "But we're not playing the who's the worst mate in history game. You claimed me, you wanted me not thirty minutes ago so what's changed? Tell me!"

"Oh, fuck." Hades closed his eyes. There was a sob in his voice which Ali's gut immediately responded to. "Nothing's changed. It's just... You're just... You're sheer perfection in every way and I'm nothing but a washed-up god barely anyone worshipped even when they did know I existed."

"Then I'm the perfect match for you, don't you see? Because in my eyes, you're perfect too."

"I'm the total opposite of perfect." Ali knew his mate was seriously upset when he found himself placed on the ground and Hades jumped to his feet. "In just our first day you've had to cope with the dread Persephone, the horrors of the pits, and now Baby's visit as well."

"This is my life, don't you see?" Hades pointed in the direction of the pits. "Those punishments you saw being inflicted on those souls there – that was my doing. My sick ideas. How can anyone, god or man, tie themselves to an evil bastard like myself, especially when their soul is as pure as yours. It's not right, it's not fair on you. Damn it, can't you see how wrong I am for you?"

Whoa. Outside of the bedroom this was the most passion Ali had seen in his new mate. And while every cell in his body urged Ali to leap up and fight back, he wasn't sure that's what Hades needed to hear. His mate's insecurities were millennia in the making and weren't going to go away with a few well-thought out phrases.

I've got to be casual about this. He checked his nails, flicking a piece of dirt out from under one of them. "So, you're giving up on me, is that it?" Ali couldn't look at Hades. If he did, he was sure he would break into a million pieces. "You've decided our mating was a mistake, the Fates got it wrong, and you're going to condemn me to eternity without love, sex, affection or anything else a shifter like myself needs to stay happy. Is that what you're saying?"

"I didn't say that exactly. What?"

Yeah. I thought that would catch your attention. Ali shrugged. It looked good when Baby did it, so he'd thought he'd give it a try. "Well, you know, touch. It's a shifter thing. That's why I used to hang around with Claude at least once a month. Chipmunks are used to being in a scurry. Scurry members are physically affectionate with each other at least in furry form. Personally, I'm surprised my parents touched each other long enough to conceive me, if truth be told, but still, Claude being a wolf used to understand that sometimes I need to be held. He gives good hugs."

Hades snarled. Ali kept his head down to hide the smirk he knew was hovering around his lips. "Claude's mated to my brother."

"Uh huh." Ali nodded. "He can't hug me as long as he used to, but there's a lot of subs at the club that don't mind a snuggle once in a while. But that's beside the point. I'm marked now." He rubbed the tattoo on his neck, hoping Hades didn't notice the shiver that brief touch elicited. "I can't get my affection or love, or sex, from anyone else ever again. Someone else touching me in a sexual manner would make me ill. I mean the same applies to you too, but from what Baby was implying, that shouldn't be a problem on your side of things. But for me, it's a big deal."

Ali stood up, brushing the grass off the back of his pants. "But no worries. I'll cope, just like I cope with every other rejection in my life. I'm not going to try and change your mind. I respect you too much for that. For the record, I don't believe in the whole 'it's not you, it's me speech,' but if that's what you're saying, that's what you think."

He looked around. The fields below the cliff were really pretty, but the rest of the landscape was pretty bleak. It's not as though there was a sign anywhere proclaiming, 'Mortal world this way'. He glanced up at Hades, managing a half smile. "Is there any way you can zap me back to Claude's without taking me yourself? I know you're not comfortable around a lot of people and when Claude hears what's happened, he's not going to be very happy with you. I can get to my place from there and just keep existing I suppose, seeing as I'm immortal now too."

"You. You're leaving me?" Hades visibly crumbled before his eyes.

"Well, what do you expect me to do? You're gutted you're mated to someone like me. I'm not going to stick around if you've got that kind of attitude. Words have power, babe." Ali took a step closer, his inner chipmunk ready to camp out on Hades' shoulder and never leave. "I can't fight your lifetime of insecurities. I understand them, I know why you have them, but I told you in plain English that you're perfect for me, insecurities and all. If you don't believe me. If you don't trust me to tell the truth about my feelings for you, then our relationship will never work. We'll be fighting about this every time you have a bad day forever more, and neither one of us want that."

"No," Hades choked out. "I don't want that either, but, it's just…." He trailed off, his chest heaving, his fists opening and closing as though he didn't know what to do.

Ali stepped closer again, just a little bit. "What type of mate did you think you'd find when you were looking all that time? Who, realistically, has lived a life like yours and can accept the horrors here with a smile on their face? Who did you imagine when you dreamed of finding your light?"

"You?" Hades looked up, so hesitant and yet so sincere.

"Then you kinda need to accept me the way I am and understand the Fates knew what they were doing." Ali closed the distance between them, laying his hand on Hades' chest. "I accept you, Hades, Lord of the Underworld, exactly the way you are, warts, horrors, ex-wives, and tortures included. Do you believe me, or are you going to call me a liar?"

"I want to believe."

"And do you accept, that if the Fates thought I was perfect for you, then you'd be perfect for me too?"

Hades nodded, staring at where Ali's hand was laying.

"And maybe next time you start to doubt your worth to me, you'll simply ask me for a hug, and I'll give you one?"

"Please." Hades' whisper carried across the barren plains.

Ali didn't hold back. Wrapping his arms around Hades' waist, he hung on tight, hating how his mate's body shook with repressed emotion, but loving the feel of Hades' arms around his shoulders. "We're going to be all right," Ali said softly. "You just have to trust what I say, instead of those annoying voices in your head."

"How did you… How did you know what was happening?"

"I hear them too," Ali said simply. He held on for the longest moment, resting his head on the chest in front of him, listening to Hades' heart, hearing his breath finally slow and move in sync with his. When he was sure his mate had calmed down, he looked up. "Our first fight," he grinned. "We get to have make up sex now. Are you up for it?" From the bulge pressing into his stomach, Ali already knew the answer to that, and he couldn't be happier about it. If anything was guaranteed to shut up those annoying voices in Hades' head, it was passion and Ali had oodles of that.

Chapter Fourteen

Hades wasn't used to any emotional turmoil. He'd learned to squash anything known as feelings back when Zeus pulled him out of his father's belly. Given domain over the Underworld, purely because his brothers didn't want it, he quickly learned his name and everything about him would be tarred by the domain he ruled.

And so it was, for more time than any mortal could count. Numb, emotionless, he often felt he existed in a vacuum until he risked sweeping Persephone off her feet. When that attempt at a relationship failed spectacularly, Hades locked his emotions in a tight steel box in his chest...

And they stayed locked away until Ali sat on his hand. As Hades laid Ali down on the grass, conjuring a spell so none could see or hear them, he could only wonder at the fact that when Ali stood calmly and asked to leave, the shriek of his soul drowned out any of the negativity he'd suffered over the years. He didn't have words – hell, he was sure he came across as a bumbling fool half the time, thanks to his social inadequacies. But he could show Ali with his touch how much the tiny chipmunk had come to mean to him in just one day.

Ali's skin was an addiction already. Slightly slick, thanks to the heated air, it rippled under his fingers as Hades gently pulled his mate's shirt over his head. He could blink, he could click his fingers, he could just think about his mate being naked and it would be so. But today, more than anything, Hades wanted to be seen as a man, not the god so many feared.

"You know I'm yours, don't you?" Bare chested and sprawled on the grass Ali was the perfect example of debauched. Hades had to wonder how he appeared to Ali as he loomed over him.

"Fates, you know how to inflame me, sweetness," Hades groaned, licking a small bead of sweat on Ali's brow and then working his lips down Ali's cheeks and under his jaw. "I want you so badly."

"Then do your magic thingy," Ali lifted his chin, giving Hades more access. Hades traced over the stark black tattoo with his tongue causing Ali to twitch and moan. "Work your magic."

"I'm trying," Hades chuckled as his lips went lower. Pert nipples begged for his attention and he gave it willingly. Ali's unique scent, the way his body responded so eagerly sent Hades' lust soaring, but he refused to rush. His mate was an angel in the body of a shifter, and he deserved every ounce of Hades' worship.

Or so he thought. But his sweet made didn't play fair. The hand shoved down the front of his pants was evidence of that. "Sweetness," he groaned against Ali's stomach. "Please."

A hand curled around his cock, tugging at it and he tried to pull back. But the touch felt so good, it just wasn't possible. Hades was many things, but stupid wasn't one of them.

Ali's lighthearted chuckle filled the air around them as his hips thrust automatically back into the hold.

Pants. Ali's pants had to go. Oh, Hades wanted to do so much more; trail a length of hot kisses down each one of his mate's legs, catch the end of Ali's cute dick in his mouth and suck on it from now until Christmas. But his sensuous mate blew his plans out of the park. He needed his cock encased in Ali's heat before he exploded.

Thank the Fates for the power of the mind. One thought, a spot of intent, because if all of Hades' thoughts became real there'd be a lot of scorched people in his family, and Ali was naked and panting, and so was he. Kneeling up, Hades brought his mate with him, Ali's legs falling on either side of his. "I need you so much," he whispered as his cock found it's home. A quick push down, Ali's work this time, not his, and Hades was in sexy heaven.

"Don't move," Hades said quickly as he felt Ali's thighs tense. "Can we just have this moment? I need…" He swallowed hard as another rush of lust hit him, "I just need to hold you like this for a second."

Slim arms wrapped around his neck, Ali's lips teasing the scar he'd left on Hades neck. Hades tried to focus on his breathing, on the pure joy that came from having his mate in his arms. There would never be another for him – that was a given without the mating factor – but in that moment, with the grass tickling his shins and the rest of his realm shut out from his senses, Hades was content. Ali had wrecked him for any other body and Hades was so damn happy he had.

But his biological functions would not be denied. Ali's chest brushed against his as he sucked and kissed his way across any of Hades' skin he could reach. There were smears on Hades' belly from Ali's cock, even the minute clenches around his own dick couldn't be ignored.

Gripping Ali's hips, Hades encouraged his willing mate to move. Slowly at first, the passion quickly caught fire between them. It was as if Hades could hear Ali's thoughts, feel his passion on a soul level and his own body responded. He didn't have them in the best of positions, Hades would have bruises on his knees by the time they were done, but he didn't care. The way Ali danced and plunged down on his cock was a sight he'd never forget.

Ali's moans and gasps were an aphrodisiac, getting higher and higher as they got caught up in the drive to come. Hades could do nothing – he couldn't move, he couldn't thrust although his hips demanded he should. The familiar ache in his belly grew, spreading down, through his groin, tightening his balls, and hardening his cock even further.

Hades gritted his teeth. He didn't want their joining to end. If he could have his way, then he and his mate would stay locked like this forever. No realm, no outside forces trying to pry them apart, just him and Ali, joined together in an act as old as history itself.

Ali's climax was his undoing. His sweet mate yelled, and plunged down, almost castrating Hades. His ass muscles tightened, and Hades couldn't move. A warm splodge exploded across his stomach, the smell of sex hitting his nostrils. Hades held onto Ali's hips and he moaned long and loud as his balls unloaded, holding Ali firmly in place as his cock poured his release into his mate.

Hades' head slumped forward, his chin resting against his mate's hair. For a long moment all that could be heard was the harsh sound of two men panting. He felt Ali turn his head, his breath puffing across Hades chest. Hades slid his hands up and across Ali's back.

He felt he should say something, anything at all, but words failed him. Hades vowed with the core of his soul that no one would take Ali away from him – not now, and not when the sun burned it's last. Ali was his, and he, in turn, belonged one hundred percent to the cute little chipmunk with the amazing personality. His whole realm could freeze over, and Hades would still be holding his mate in his arms.

Chapter Fifteen

Ali wasn't sure what to make of Baby. The guy was drop dead gorgeous, but Ali expected that of a son of Poseidon. But it was like he was two people. A public and then a more 'real' persona and Ali wasn't sure which one was honest.

Hades had elected for them to have dinner in what he called his private dining suite. Forty people could easily have sat around the table, although at least the three of them were sitting in one corner of it. Ali's fingers itched to add some color to the stark room. His mate had left this room off his earlier tour. *Definitely later,* he promised himself.

The thick black velvet curtains had been ordered closed by Hades the moment they'd entered the room. There was a roaring fire in the huge fireplace that took up one half of a wall. One large central chandelier shone over the table, throwing gray shadows onto the black walls. Ali wouldn't have thought the gray on black was possible until he saw it himself, but he put that down to an Underworld quirk. Ali noticed a few of those quirks, like the shadows, the way the walls seemed to breathe, how the demons never looked Hades in the eye, and Baby's behavior.

Ali watched, eyes narrowing slightly. Baby was chatting to Hades about Artemas, who Ali gathered was a brother. He'd never spent a lot of time talking to Poseidon, so he wasn't sure of the family dynamics at play. Baby had apparently spent time with Artemas and his mate after something or other happened. Ali wasn't paying attention to the details. He was watching Baby as Folsom came in, carrying a large bottle of wine. The gods could certainly scull through their alcohol.

There it was, the moment Baby knew Folsom was in the room. The god's posture changed instantly. Instead of leaning over the table, as he was talking to Hades, Baby leaned back in his chair, spread his legs and hooked a thumb into his belt loop. Tilting his head back, he sent his hair shimmering like a wave over his shoulders. Baby's eyelids half closed, and a half-smile curved his full lips.

Folsom, being who he was, focused his attention on Hades. "This is the last bottle of the twenty-two," he said, popping the cork with a flourish. "If you needed me to, I could go topside...."

"That will be all, Folsom," Hades growled. If he noticed the change in Baby's demeanor, he didn't say anything. "Ask Mavis to bring in the dessert trolley and then leave us."

Folsom rolled his eyes, but scurried out of the room. The moment he left, Baby went back to leaning his arms on the table again.

"Why do you do that?" Ali knew Folsom couldn't be Baby's mate. The young godling did the same thing when the female servers were at the table serving the main course. Any time anyone was around, Baby sat back looking like sex on a stick.

"Do what?" Baby turned his head with a smile. "Pose, you mean?" He laughed. "Don't let it upset you. I don't mean anything by it. People expect me to be sex personified, regardless of what species they are. Isn't that right, Uncle?"

"You are your own person, Baby," Hades said softly. "Just because both of your fathers were raging nymphos doesn't mean you have to be. Sei changed his behavior, so can you."

The smile fell off Baby's face. "I don't know how to be anyone else. My gods, just being around Himeros...."

"Hang on a minute." Ali's brain finally caught up with the conversation. "Are you suggesting your other father was Himeros? The Greek god of desire?" He learned about male gods having babies when Poseidon was pregnant, so he wasn't shocked about that. But the god of desire giving birth?

"I'm sure that was mentioned back at the pits where we met, but yes, he is and now you see my problem." Baby shrugged. "Sei was known as a shag-master from the beginning of time. He got Himeros, the god of desire himself up the duff and I'm the result. What no one seems to understand is that none of the trouble that follows me from one freaking place to the next is my fault. Mortals, paranormals, even other gods fall all over me the moment they see me, and I'm supposed to do what? Ignore them? How am I supposed to know if they're married, or have a significant other if they're draping themselves all over me?"

"You could try having a conversation before you unzipped your pants," Hades said drily.

"Yeah, and look how that turns out for me." Baby shook his head. "That just gives more people in the same place the idea I'm worth fighting over because I'm playing hard to get. Face it, I am what I am. An unwanted bastard. Himmie couldn't get rid of me quick enough when he found he was preggers. Sei was too busy filling his own bed with random nobodies to ever pay attention to me growing up. If it wasn't for my brothers, I'd probably have been a foundling growing up with wolves or something equally depressing."

"At least you had someone on your side growing up," Ali said hesitantly. The bit he knew about Poseidon's history came from the man himself and Baby had barely been mentioned. "Your brothers must care for you."

"They're all busy with their own mates now," Baby scoffed. "You know, I thought Sei was bad before, but now he's had the twins, he's suddenly decided to become father of the year. Insisting I stick with him, babysit the twins, don't go out, don't go messing with Claude's blessed wolves. For fuck's sake, I'm over a thousand years old. I know how to behave, it's others that don't."

"I thought you'd been spending time with Himeros." Hades flashed Ali a reassuring smile. Sweet, but not helpful. Ali got the impression Baby was on the verge of a temper tantrum.

"He's worse!" Baby pushed back his chair. "He didn't have anything at all to do with me when I was a kid, right? Nothing. Nada. He gave birth, shoved me in Sei's direction and took off, blaming me for his stretch marks. Now, all of a sudden since Sei met Claude, he wants to be my bosom buddy. Lure that guy in, Baby, see if you can get into that woman's pants over there, Baby, prove how much you're my son. Let's see if we can upset Zeus, Baby, and start a gang bang on fucking Olympus."

The last word was shouted. Baby was on his feet, his fist smacking across his chest. "There has to be more to me, right? I have to have some value to someone, surely, besides what my dick or mouth can do. Someone, somewhere must see me as something more than a sex machine."

The sadness in Baby's rant was heart wrenching. "Baby, please, sit down," Ali said gently. "You know we don't expect anything from you here. Maybe we can help?"

"No disrespect, little Unc," Baby said scornfully, "but you couldn't have any idea what it was like growing up as me. The only thing you've ever had to worry your little head about was finding nuts. Oh yeah," his laugh was harsh. "Maybe we do have something in common after all. That's all I ever find too, is nuts. No, no," he added as Hades stood up. "I know. No dissing the mates. I'm going. Thanks for dinner. See you in the next millennium or so."

He disappeared with a flashbang that made Ali jump. "I didn't mean to make him go," he said urgently. "I was just trying to help him feel better. He was so upset. Where will he go now?"

Hades had been standing, staring at the spot on the floor Baby disappeared from. At Ali's questioning, he gave himself a small shake, and looked over, his smile sad. "Gods have never made the best parents," he said, "not that I've seen anyway. Sei was better than most, he had four of his sons living with him, out of goodness knows how many offspring, but he never did much beyond giving them food and shelter. Himeros was a nightmare and now Baby is suffering because of them both."

"There must be some good ones, out there." Ali wriggled out of his seat and hurried to his mate's side. He was starting to recognize the 'I need a hug' look. "Demeter must have really cared about Persephone or she wouldn't have been so upset when you took her."

From the way Hades shook his head, Ali wished he'd picked another example. "Demeter was 'sad' and yes that word should be in inverted comments, because Persephone's abduction took her out of her control. I'm not saying there isn't some motherly love involved, but a lot about what Demeter did at that time was about control. Why do you think Persephone insisted on remaining queen down here even though she couldn't stand the sight of me?"

Ali sighed. "I'm sorry, I should never have brought her up as an example. I forgot you'd already told me that was about control and Persephone wanting to be higher ranked than her mother. But surely there must be some good parents among the gods? Maybe, someone who could help Baby get through whatever he is going through now?"

"You have such a caring soul." Ali found his feet dangling, as Hades caught him up and twirled him around. "I'm so lucky to have been blessed with you."

That didn't answer my question, but then Ali forgot there was a question when Hades' lips took control of his. There was a stray thought, one hoping Baby would be okay, that might have found its way to the Fates, but Ali wasn't sure if that's how life worked, and he was too busy being seduced to think clearly.

Chapter Sixteen

Hades woke up, curled around his mate which was fast becoming his favorite thing to do in any realm. But even as his brain kicked into gear, he knew it wasn't a day for smiling, as he'd been prone to do more often lately. Nope. Today was court day – the day when the souls deemed too evil to live among the general populations in his realm had to face the Lord of the Underworld and be given their punishment in person. Something Hades had been putting off for two days in favor of spending time with Ali.

He looked down at his sleeping mate. Ali was curled up, his hair in disarray, one hand resting over his mating tattoo while the other was resting on Hades' hip. *Such a sweet and sensual soul,* he thought fondly, tucking one of Ali's curls behind his ear. In the two days since Baby left, they'd toured the Underworld and made changes to his huge mansion. Ali charmed demons and souls alike. The hounds all thought he was adorable, wanting to sniff him all the time, and growling at any soul who got too close, and the demon children clamored to be picked up anytime Ali was near.

The only being living in Hades' domain who didn't like Ali was Cerberus. *Damn dog's going to be put down if he can't learn to behave himself,* Hades thought as he remembered how Cerberus had lunged at Ali when introduced, the teeth on all three heads gnashing together when the chain he was on stopped the dog from making contact.

Ali was shaken, understandably so, especially when Cerberus kept trying to attack even after Hades forced him to stand down. Hades didn't have it in him to destroy the pup he'd raised since Cerberus came into being, but he had to wonder if Lasse's comments months before about Cerberus being jealous of any one he was with had some basis of truth.

Cerberus had adored Persephone, drooling after her every time she came to visit, hanging on her heels like a devoted puppy. But when Lasse told Cerberus months before, that Hades was actively searching for a mate, Cerberus lost the plot at him, Jason, and Thor. Ignoring the jealousy angle, Hades had punished Cerberus and his brother for trying to take over the Underworld, but he couldn't keep Cerberus locked up indefinitely. Cerberus's brother was already licking his singed fur in the fires of Tartarus for his part in the bid for power and Lasse's abduction. At the time, it was only Cerberus's begging and constant reminders over how loyal he was, that kept him out of the fires too. *But that won't last if he doesn't accept my mate.*

Hades knew he was procrastinating. Cerberus would either redeem himself or he wouldn't and dwelling on it wasn't going to change anything. The thing was, it was really hard to get himself in the mood for being the bad ass he needed to be on court day when all he wanted to do was listen to Ali's cute snuffles as he slept, or stroke those curls, or.... *That's not helping.*

What Hades should be doing is sneaking out. It's what he'd planned. Sneak out, do one of the rottenest parts of his job, and be back in time for a late breakfast. He clothed himself with a quick thought, eager to get the horrible part of his day over and done with, but the flutter of Ali's eye lashes even as he went to remove his mate's hand from his hip, let Hades know he'd been caught.

"You're already dressed." Propping himself up on his elbow, Ali brushed his curls off his face. "Give me two seconds to use the bathroom, and I'll be right with you." He smiled, so open and pure, Hades' heart ached. "Looks like serious stuff going on today, am I right?" Leaning up, Ali pecked Hades on the cheek and then rolled out of the other side of the bed.

"I was thinking," he called out from the bathroom, "if we get the chance, can we pop back to Claude's later today? I need my keys and phone, and I was thinking we could pop around to my house." There was a sound of the tap running. Seconds later Ali came out, still wiping his face with a towel.

"I don't need much from my place," he said, his lovely smile still in place. "But I'd probably better empty my refrigerator. I've got milk and things in there that are probably planning a revolution as we speak. Did you want to clothe me?" He dropped his towel and opened his arms. "Or will the clothes you gave me yesterday do?"

Hades bit the inside of his gum. Naked Ali was totally gorgeous and stirring parts of his anatomy that had no place in his throne room. It didn't help that Ali's cock was already plumping up. "I have court day today," Hades said quickly, climbing off the bed in an effort to distract himself. "You could go to Claude's if you like and I'll meet you there later?"

"Something somber and suitably Lord-like then," Ali sighed. "Do your worst, but not black. Black clothing makes me look like an underfed vampire. Oh, I know. How about something different. Like, maybe a kilt, and some boots, and something ruggedly manly for the top half. What do you think?"

"You could go to Claude's?" Hades said half-heartedly. He already knew Ali wouldn't leave his side. His mate was the epitome of sweet and stubborn. He sighed. "You'd suit a kilt. You've got the legs for it. How about this?"

Flicking his fingers in Ali's direction, Hades couldn't help but smile at his mate's delighted reaction. The kilt was pink and mauve, hanging at regulation length just below the middle of Ali's knees. The sporran sported Hades' marks in silver, done in the softest black leather that matched Ali's new knee high biker boots. For a top, Hades pictured a close fitting Henley in a dark green, that provided a bit of contrast with Ali's leather coat that matched his.

"I look bad ass," Ali crowed, twirling around. "You are so good to me," he added running across the room. Hades already had his arms open. Catching his mate as he leaped was never a hardship. He only wished the day's events wouldn't wipe the smile of Ali's face – although he knew it would.

/~/~/~/~/

It was an hour later before Hades led Ali down the long corridor to his throne room, his dream of having a leisurely breakfast brought to a halt by Folsom's incessant demands while they were trying to eat. His PA was madly organized, but he had no idea of personal space, or Hades' desire for a private meal with his mate. After the sixth such interruption, where Folsom plonked some papers beside his plate to be signed, Hades gave up on his sausages, eggs and chips. Ali had finished his meal and that was his main concern.

"Give us a minute." Hades stopped by the throne room door and held his finger up in front of Folsom's face. "In fact, get the demon guards in place but no one is to come in here for ten minutes. Got that?" He resisted the urge to flick the demon's nose.

"Yes, oh Lord and Master. March the demons to the door. Don't open door for ten minutes, starting now."

Shaking his head, Hades opened one side of the door in front of him, ushering Ali through and closing it firmly behind him. The room had never changed in all the time he'd been in charge of the Underworld. It was designed to scare the hardest soul which meant it was still as stark as ever. The only light came from the fire pit, which cast an orange flickering glow over the bone thrones. Hades was pleased to see the cushions he'd conjured for Ali were still on his seat.

"Remember," he said, as he took Ali's hand, and walked them across the room. "You don't have to say anything, or do anything. Just try not to get too upset at anything I might say or do."

"I know who you are inside," Ali promised, turning and resting his head on Hades' chest. "You know,

223

you're making a big deal out of this. You'll sentence a few evil souls to eternal torment, then we'll go to Claude's. We might make it there for lunch?"

"For dinner, definitely." Hades appreciate the fact Ali was trying to make light of things for him, but he hadn't had a court sitting in well over a week. The cells were backed up and needed to be cleared. But he would take time to kiss his mate, because Ali was trying so hard to fit in.

"Okay then," Ali said some five minutes later as he wiggled his butt on his throne. Hades felt a shaft of pride that his lips and cheeks were the same color as the pink on his kilt. "What if I do want to say something? Is it allowed?"

"Ask questions you mean?" Hades lowered himself into his throne, and called on his power. "My sweet, you can say anything you like at any time. All you need to remember is that it's the weight of a person's soul that's brought them here, and no matter what words come out of their mouths, that doesn't change. That's what I sentence them on - their actions and the amount of darkness in their souls. Nothing can ever excuse a darkness on a person's soul."

"But what if a person's murdered someone, but it was self-defense?"

"Sweetheart, our system is not like the justice system you are used to on earth. A self-defense murder won't leave a black mark on an individual's soul. Believe me, this system is as old as time itself. It accounts for the intent of a person when they do their evil deeds. Earth laws as such, have nothing to do with it. Remember, we are sentencing souls – and a soul can't lie to itself."

"These are all bad people. Got it." Ali grinned and gave him the thumbs up. Hades could feel a headache forming across the top of his eyes. *My mate is too good to be here. I should call this off,* but once again he was too late. Folsom had already opened the door and the first dozen souls were dragged by their chains into the room.

Chapter Seventeen

Ali was tired, slightly nauseated and with every passing minute he was feeling more and more sorry for Hades. All the souls, without exception, believed there were extenuating circumstances that landed them in the darkest court across all realms. Ali had been amusing himself, wondering what type of label a psychiatrist would give to the hordes of faces that made their way across the marble floors before being forced to kneel at Hades' feet.

Psychopaths.

Sociopaths.

Obsessives.

Sadists, and not the consensual sexual kind.

Fanatics.

Murderers.

Pedophiles. Ali didn't dare move when the Furies arrived to take them away, just as Hades had said they would.

Ali zoned out as Folsom announced the last group. It really didn't matter what society called those black souls – they were all guilty of evil acts against other people; some of them that made Ali's stomach revolt when Folsom read out the crimes from a long scroll. Paranormal or human, it didn't matter. It was as if the part of their brain that was meant to show empathy or caring for other people was completely absent in the sentenced souls. This was evident in the number of the wretched beings who tried to "do a deal" with Hades as though he was the devil and they would gladly submit to his command – just so they could grab the chance to hurt more people.

I don't know how he does it, Ali mused. Upright in his chair, Hades exuded control, and a darkness that could be felt by everyone. Not one joke passed between the demons guarding the souls. Folsom didn't smile once, and Ali didn't dare. Not that he felt like smiling anyway. All he could think was his poor mate was forced to listen to crime after crime, followed by a litany of lies falling from the mouths of accused.

Don't these guys get it? Ali thought as he watched one man fling out his arms and yell, "I made it, Ma. I'm in hell just like you said I'd be," as he was dragged before Hades by one of the guards. And then the same man laughed as though his whole life had been one big joke and death was nothing more than the next part of his great adventure. The crimes Folsom read out on his behalf were nothing to laugh at though, and the man didn't think his situation was quite so funny when Hades ordered him sent to the pits to be ripped apart by two demon bulls who never got tired and who could happily keep tearing the man's limbs from his body every time they joined up again, which, according to Hades would occur every five minutes – for the next four thousand, seven hundred and sixty years. Apparently, the extent of the man's crimes meant he ranked at the very highest spot on Folsom's flowchart.

Not long to go now. Ali was already thinking about how he could help his stressed mate feel better.

"Thorndike Garcia," Folsom intoned.

Ali's head shot up. He stared as a non-descript man in a smart suit was dragged to Hades' feet and shoved to his knees by the accompanying demon. The man had clearly never kneeled in front of someone before, as he kept trying to lift his head. Ali winced as a hard smack around the man's skull, forced his nose onto the marble.

"Thorndike Garcia, you have been brought before Hades, Lord of the Underworld, to answer for your crimes of human trafficking, enslaving innocents, profiting from human misery and murdering your bonded mate, Lucy," Folsom read with a flourish.

"You killed Aunt Lucy?" Ali slapped his hand across his mouth, as Hades looked at him sharply.

"This man is a relative of yours?" Hades asked as Thorndike tried to struggle out of the demon hold, he was in.

"My uncle, well, sort of. He was my grandfather's brother. He and Aunt Lucy…." Ali broke off, his mind swamped with images of a happier time back when he was a child. Huge barbecues with hundreds of extended family members, trips to the beach, staying at Uncle Thorn's house. His father's voice wafted through his mind – *why can't you be more like your Uncle Thorn? Now, there's a man who's made a success of himself without kissing ass with wolves.* "It's nothing," he said quickly, "Carry on. Forget I spoke."

"Ali, mate," Hades said quietly. "If you'd rather leave…."

"Ali?" Thorndike shrieked, twisting his head to peer up at the thrones. "Is that Braydon's welp? The idiot who saved a wolf and thought his shit didn't stink anymore? The one no one in the scurry hasn't had anything to do with for the past eighty odd years because he's nothing but a weak loser. Let me up, you asshole."

Hades waved his hand at the demon, causing him to back up. "Are you referring to my mate and consort in those derogatory terms?" he asked, his words dropping like ice in the overly hot room, as Thorndike struggled to his feet.

"Just telling the truth, aren't I," Thorndike sneered, smoothing down his rumpled suit jacket. "The fact that boy's sitting there, in a skirt no less, with a red cushion to protect his skinny ass, proves the boy is dead, the same as me, and the only reason he's being kept around is because the rumors about him taking a cock up his ass must be true. One would've thought the Lord of the Underworld could do so much better for himself."

The room was suddenly filled with the sound of twenty demons growling and snapping their teeth. Ali chewed the corner of his lip as the sound got louder, but one click of Hades' fingers and the sound abruptly stopped.

Ali watched as Hades stood and reached out his hand to him. Still dazed, and more than a little ashamed of his uncle's words, Ali took it, allowing himself to be pulled to his feet. He felt like a dwarf as Hades grew into his more frightening form.

"I am the Lord of the Underworld." Hades' voice boomed around the room. "The worst of the demons jump to attention when they hear my name. Hellhounds howl when they hear my roar and they hunt on my behalf; hunt for all eternity to render those souls who disrespect me and mine to nothing but bite-sized chunks of food."

"Hades, babe, I think my uncle got the message," Ali whispered, tugging on Hades' pants which was the only part he could reach when his mate was in his godly form. "How about you just get to the eternal punishment bit, and we'll go have something to eat, aye?"

"Punishment?" Thorndike looked shocked. "Isn't being dead enough? I've got a dozen deals that'll all fall through because some shit poisoned my stroganoff. There's Lucy's funeral to arrange, I've got...."

"Nothing," Hades snarled. "You've got nothing, because you're very much dead and you're going to stay that way. Unlike Ali who's not only alive, but thanks to being my mate is now co-ruler of the Underworld and immortal with it. He'll have a life of joy and luxury that I will provide. All you have to look forward to is an eternity of pain and torment."

Ali could tell the instant Hades' words had penetrated his uncle's skull. Shock quickly followed by a calculating grin.

"We're family, boy." Thorndike opened his arms. Ali leaned closer to his mate's leg. "Surely, you've got something down here a man of my talents can do that doesn't involve the whole pain and torment side of things?"

"That's not how it works, Uncle," Ali said, empowered by a thick finger drifting over his hair. "My mate has a very important job. It's his duty to protect the living from the likes of you. The black marks on your soul don't lie."

"But that was up there," Thorndike waved his hand at the ceiling. "I'm not stupid enough to think I can escape being dead. But Fates willing, I'll reincarnate soon enough, and, in the meantime, there must be some financial or managerial role you can swing for me to keep me comfortable till then. After all, there are some things I know about you, I'm sure your oversized mate would prefer I kept quiet about."

Ali froze in horror, Hades' words when they first came to the realm ringing through his head. *Never let anyone know your true name.* He glanced up, but Hades didn't seem worried. In fact, there was a small smile hovering on his huge lips.

"You think to make a deal with me, mortal?"

"I'm sure we can come to some arrangement," Thorndike puffed out his chest. "I realize not even someone with your power can send me back to the realm of the living, but I can keep my mouth shut about some things, if you make it worth my while. And, and," he added, casting a look up at Hades, "remember even if you shut my mouth permanently, I can still write, tap out a message with my toes, scratch out my secrets in blood if that's what it takes."

Ali twisted his hands. His uncle would make good on his threat. In all his years of life, he'd never heard of Thorndike Garcia losing a deal, or failing to get his way.

"You present me with an interesting challenge." Hades smiled openly this time. "You know, my mate," Ali tilted his neck so he could see Hades' face. "I recall you mentioned that driving through the pits was probably easier than sitting down at one of your family's dinner parties. I think I have to agree."

"My uncle has had his own way a long time," Ali admitted quietly, shame flooding every cell in his body at the things his family member might say.

"Usually, when I devise a punishment for a soul as black as yours," Hades said in the same tone of voice he'd use to discuss the weather, "I'd make a point of insisting the soul relive every pain and torment they've caused others, time, after time, after time. It's a form of karma, what I do. A way of ensuring that those souls whom the Fates have turned away from, will spend every second of eternity wishing they'd done something different with their last shot of life."

Thorndike frowned. "The Fates allow for reincarnation of every shifter soul – it's a way of ensuring true mates can be reunited even after death."

"But you didn't take up with your true mate, did you?" Hades tilted his head to one side, slightly. His voice still boomed around the room, but Ali could listen to it for hours. "Let me see, ah, there it is, tucked away in the deepest darkest spot of your memory banks. A young lad, aww... such a sweet soul, destined by the Fates to be your mate and you flatly rejected him, like so many in your scurry have done over the years when the mate chosen from them doesn't fit the family ideals."

It was Ali's turn to frown. He knew very few of his scurry were fated mate couples, but he'd never heard of anyone rejecting one.

But Thorndike seemed pleased. "Darren. Is he here? I heard he'd died not long after we split up. That would be a blessed relief, to see him again. The Fates couldn't ignore our chance at reincarnation if we're both here together."

"His heart was broken." The humor fell off Hades' face, his expressionless mask falling in its place. He closed his eyes, as though listening for a moment. "Darren was never meant for a place like this. His soul was too pure and sweet for that. The Fates reincarnated him swiftly, he's already been bound to another for over a hundred years. The Fates have a message for you – very unusual in these circumstances, but there you are. I can let you know Darren is blissfully happy. I imagine the Fates have interceded this time, probably to torment you because you will never find a moment's happiness again."

"Darren's got someone else? But, when he died, I felt sure…."

"That you could manipulate the Fates to your way of thinking," Hades growled. "Guess what, asshole, you're shit out of luck. If you'd just walked away, let Darren die of natural causes, then maybe you were right, and your chance at an eternal mate might have been granted, but you didn't just let Darren die, did you? You shot him point blank in the head and then pulled out his heart and tossed it in the gutter to make sure he couldn't embarrass you."

"Uncle. No!" Ali couldn't believe what he was hearing.

"What would you know about how things were back then," Thorndike said angrily. "I couldn't have a male mate; I'd have never done business with anyone respectable again. How was I meant to have kids if I was stuck with a mate with the same plumbing I've got? For fuck's sake, think logically about it."

The problem was, Ali could see his uncle believed everything he said. His mind again was filled with images, but this time it was his Aunt Lucy's harried face he saw – the lines around her eyes and mouth, the way she always looked away or found something else to do when her bond mate was around. Burying his nose against Hades' thigh, Ali inhaled sharply.

"Please get the sentencing over and done with, my mate. I've coped with all I can today."

"I'll be a danger to you and your mating every second I'm down here," Thorndike yelled. "Ali will never be safe, and you can't kill me. You'll never keep me quiet. You've no idea what I can do and what's so funny is, you can't do anything to me that will stop me spilling my secrets. I'm already dead!"

"Which means you don't need to breathe, now, doesn't it?" Hades flickered his fingers and Ali watched as water flowed from somewhere, puddling around his uncle's ankles, and rising up his legs. As it got higher, ice began to form. Thorndike's thins lips turned blue.

"Water is more my brother's domain than mine," Hades said as the ice got higher and Thorndike's upper half started to shiver. "But we can all borrow tricks from each other if we like." The water was rising faster now, over Thorndike's groin and seeping up his chest.

"You see, most people think there is a downside of using ice as a means of restraint," Hades continued in the same tone, "In its usual form it can be melted or shattered, and you're probably thinking you'll be able to get someone to free you. But this is no ordinary water. It comes from the rivers that circle my domain. It will never melt."

The water had reached Thorndike's chin. He was trying to say something, but his teeth were chattering so hard, he couldn't make his mouth work properly.

"This ice will never melt," Hades repeated, "and should by some twist of fate, your body and the ice surrounding it shatters, it will reform, exactly as it is now. Your secrets," he added as the ice flowed up Thorndike's face, "Will be locked away for eternity, just like you will be."

Ali buried his head in Hades' thigh. He heard a gasp, or maybe it was a moan, but he ignored it, squeezing his eyes tightly shut. All he was conscious of was Hades' hand, cupping his head, holding him firmly, offering him comfort, even when Ali thought there was none to be had.

"And it is done," Hades said, about a minute later. "Folsom, this one will remain in the fires of Tartarus. Make sure the guards know my consort should never have his eyes defiled by this sight again, or they will share the same fate."

"Gladly, my Lord. Guards take the remaining few souls back to their cells," Folsom said crisply. "The Lord and his consort need time to themselves. These wretches can ponder their fate for another week. Will there be anything else, my Lord, consort?"

Pushing himself upright, Ali tilted his chin, watching as two huge guards pushed the ice cube that used to be his uncle towards the fire pit. His uncle's face was twisted in horror, his eyes wide, his mouth twisted in disbelief. Hardening his heart, Ali watched in silence, refusing to move until the ice cube disappeared down into the pits.

Only when he was sure his uncle was truly gone, Ali turned to Folsom. "My mate and I would like a meal served in our private quarters as quickly as possible. We'll be returning to Tulsa later today and I'm not sure how long we will be gone. No more than a few days at most. In the meantime, please ensure the guards get extra treats in their meals tonight, and if you could keep things running smoothly until our return, it would be much appreciated. You all do a fantastic job. Thank you."

A rumble of surprise ran among the remaining demons, but for the first time that day, Ali saw true smiles on their ugly faces. Folsom too, seemed stunned at being thanked, but he recovered quickly. "Of course, my Lord, thank you Consort," he said bowing as he left the room. "All hail the Lord of the Underworld and his benevolent consort."

Reaching up, Ali took Hades' hand, and stepped off the dais, and headed towards the door. *I will not break, I will be worthy,* he told himself firmly as the rousing cheers from the demons followed them out of the throne room.

Chapter Eighteen

Hades should have known it would be inevitable, now Ali was granted with immortal life, that at some point in his time in the Underworld, Ali might come across someone he knew, or was related to. Hades just didn't realize it would happen on his very first court day. Of all the damn bad luck, or it would have been if the Fates hadn't picked that day to let Hades know they were present – in his realm, and in his head.

Hades almost shit himself when he heard the foreign voice wafting through his mind like it belonged there. A voice he quickly recognized although it'd been eons since the Fates had spoken to him. They worked through Thanatos as a rule. But it gave him a warm feeling, a sense that his lengthy prayers to the Fates for a mate hadn't been ignored all those years. They'd just been biding their time, waiting for the right time and as Fate would have it, they were keeping an eye on Ali too.

Which was amazingly comforting. But Hades was at a bit of a loss as to what to say to Ali now. Sentencing Thorn to an eternity of silence, with nothing but the thoughts in his sick brain for company probably wasn't mentioned in the "Good Mates Guide." Ali wasn't helping – his back ramrod straight as they strode through the corridors to their private apartments. Their joined hands were their only connection.

But Hades had to say something. He had to know if what he'd done had ruined their connection forever. "Ali," he said softly, as Ali pushed open the huge double doors to their living space.

"Give me a minute," Ali warned. "I'm not angry at you, pissed off at you, or upset with what you did. I just need a minute to process everything."

That didn't help. 'Everything' could mean anything and everything. Hades allowed his form to resume his human size and hurried over to the bar in the corner of the room. Their living space was a lot more comfortable now, thanks to Ali, and filled with bright color. But Hades insisted the bar stay black. He privately liked how the glasses glistened against the marble. Pouring Ali a small drink and himself a larger one, he took the glasses over to where Ali was sitting in the middle of the new couch.

"Got room for me?" He asked, handing Ali his drink.

Hades felt Ali's sigh right down to his toes, but his heart stuttered when Ali patted the place beside him. Sitting down, rather stiffly because Hades wasn't sure what was going to happen, he was surprised when Ali swung around, resting his leg on the cushions as if he wanted to see Hades' face.

"I promise you, I'm not mad at you, or angry, or upset, or any other word you can come up with, that I can see written on your handsome face. You do a damn hard job and I don't think I appreciated how hard it was until I saw what you went through today."

What I went through? All I do is sit on a throne and dole out punishments. Hades took a gulp of his drink. Ali was a chatty chipmunk, maybe he'd explain a bit more.

"You have to listen to that shit day in, day out. Don't you ever get tired of it?"

Hades went with a half shrug. "It is my job."

"Well, it's a damn rotten job, if you ask me," Ali said hotly. "Seriously, I know I've said it before, but I think you got the bum end of a bad deal. Zeus sits around in his clouds all day, fucking anything that moves and never having to deal with anything remotely mortal. When Poseidon visits his realm all he has to contend with is oil slicks and over friendly krakens, and while the oil is horrible, at least it doesn't talk back."

"Eternity is a long time, sweetness." Hades tried to explain. "The souls down here don't have a chance of reincarnation, or going to heaven or anything like that, except in the rarest of cases. While there is nothing they can say that would mitigate the sentences I give them, I feel it is part of my duty to hear them out."

"Are you really sure you have to?" Hades' heart warmed at the way his mate peered up at him, an earnest expression on his face. "Only, I have to say, yeah, innocent until proven on earth, but these guys are only down here because their souls are weighted down with their misdeeds. You told me that. And today could've gone a lot faster if you'd sewn their mouths shut before they were on their knees."

"It's the last chance they have to speak," Hades said although his mate was right. "Surely, I owe them that?"

"But you just said it didn't make any difference what those souls said anyway." Ali started jiggling in his seat. "I know, I know. These souls spend time in the cells, right, before they get their audience with you?"

Hades nodded and took a smaller sip of his drink this time. He was enjoying how Ali's eyes sparkled when he got an idea.

"Well, it must be pretty boring sitting in those cells, contemplating their navel, so why don't you get forms printed up, that they can fill in and outline their defense before the court date? That way, they feel they are getting their say, and all you have to do when you see them is tell them what they're sentenced to."

"But then I'd have to read their responses." Hades liked the idea of shorting court times, but imagining himself buried under a mountain of paper didn't sound like fun.

"No, you wouldn't." Ali put his glass down on the coffee table and gripped Hades' arm. "Don't you see? Folsom or one of the guards can let them know what they are being charged with when they arrive. They can spend their time in their cells, writing out this huge defense, which you can just throw away. It's part of their torment, don't you see? They imagine they have this chance to make a deal with you, and bam, you blow that idea out of the water by sentencing them without even letting them speak."

His mate did have a creative mind and the idea had a certain appeal to it, but Ali wasn't finished.

"I mean, did you hear what that idiot was going on about, the one who'd killed and eaten his entire family and then when he got hungry, put a room to rent notice in the local paper and started eating the applicants too? He went on for over half an hour claiming he absorbed the souls of those he'd eaten, gaining extra special powers so he could work as part of his God's special plan. It was sick. I thought he was going to offer you recipes."

Unfortunately, that particular soul wasn't unusual. Hades put his glass next to Ali's and took his mate's hand. "Sweetness, that is a good idea, but I'm not sure its allowed."

"You've got rules governing what you have to do?"

"Well," Hades said slowly, "the only rule is that a being who doesn't fit into one of our general categories has to have an audience with me before he is sentenced."

"But they will still have their audience, and, and," Hades never wanted Ali to stop talking when he got excited. "Oh, I know, you can appoint a couple of demons to go through the paperwork, and if there is something you desperately should know, like there has been a genuine mistake and the soul doesn't belong down here, then they can bring that to your attention before the court day starts."

"Hon, every soul that comes down here belongs here," Hades smoothed his thumb over the back of Ali's hand. "They can't find the Underworld unless this is where they are meant to be. It's not like there's a crossroads at the point of death, with 'your heavenly rest' on one side and 'the Underworld' on the other."

"Then if they are meant to be here, there's no need for you to see all of them, or any of them." Ali put on his stubborn face. "Except you say there is a rule. Who made the rule? Who do we see about getting it changed?"

Hades eyed the door. *How much longer is Folsom going to be with our food.* "I'm not sure exactly," he said when he realized Ali wasn't going to let the subject go without an answer. "It's just the way it's always been. I mean, that's what I do. I sentence dark souls to eternal torment."

"But what if you didn't have to." Ali wiggled closer and Hades' lungs kicked up a gear. "What if we could oversee your domain from your lovely carriage, and left the sentencing to someone else. Evil is evil, no matter what that person did in life. What I heard today, there's a never-ending pattern – soul does nasty thing to someone else, or multiple someones. Soul tries to justify their actions to you which doesn't work because you've heard it all before and the marks on their soul don't lie. It really doesn't matter what they did or what you sentence them to, someone on earth suffered because of what those souls did, and this domain ensures they won't do it again. You saw over a thousand people today. How many times do you hold these court days?"

"Two or three times a week, but I haven't done any since I met you," Hades added quickly. "I usually see on average, five hundred souls a session but today was unusual."

"Have you always had to see so many?" Ali's eyes widened and Hades was conscious that he was leaning towards his sweet mate.

"No," Hades shook his head slowly. "It's gotten steadily worse over the past fifty years. In the last ten years alone, my numbers have tripled."

"Hate seems to spread faster than kindness." Ali looked down at their joined hands. "Babe, it's going to get worse. There's stuff going on... the good people are doing what they can, but you're going to be swamped before much longer."

"This realm seems to have the capacity to expand accordingly."

"But do you?" Ali insisted. "How long will it be before you're holding court sessions every day just so your cells don't overflow? How much more hate, and lying justification will you have to hear before your soul breaks?"

Hades didn't know what to say. "What are you saying, sweetness? Do you want me to give up who I am and what I do?" His breath quickened for a totally different reason this time that had nothing to do with Ali's closeness. He was the Lord of the Underworld. He had been for almost as long as time itself. If he didn't have his job, his position among the gods....

"Hades, stop." Strong hands gripped his shoulders. Hades blinked and noticed he was staring at a concerned mate. "I am not now and nor will I ever suggest you be anything than what you are. I love who you are. I'm not trying to stop you being the big wig down here. I just think you need to learn to delegate more."

"Delegate? Wait. What? You love me?" Hades could barely get the words past the sudden lump in his throat. His whole life – that's how long he'd been waiting to hear those words. "You love me already?"

"Babe," Ali's smile lit up the room, "I'm a shifter. Me and my animal half, we knew who you were to us the moment we met. You're never going to hurt me, screw around on me, or leave me. And while you don't believe it, I know you have an amazing heart, a rocking hot bod, and you're mine. What's not to love?"

"You... you... you have no idea." And of course, then, when Hades was busy trying to cope with an overflowing heart and a swamp of sensations he'd never dealt with before, there was a freaking knock on the door.

But Ali was on top of things. "Leave the tray by the door," he yelled. "We're not to be disturbed for anything."

Hades could hear Folsom muttering, but the door stayed closed. Ali crept into his arms, his soft fingers smoothing over the tear tracks on Hades' cheeks. "You've not had a lot of love in your life, have you?" He asked softly.

Shaking his head, Hades blinked rapidly. "It's been an eternity of loneliness without you."

"I'm sorry." Ali mock pouted and Hades knew his mate was trying to make him feel better. "On the plus side, seeing as you're a god, we have an eternity left to make up for it."

"I love you too." As Hades said the words it was as if a dam broke around his soul. Feelings flooded his body, not all of them his own. He gasped. "Is that...?"

"Our bond." Ali winked. "There's been a part of you closed off to me since the night you claimed me. It's okay. I understand, but damn, can you imagine how good our sex is going to be if we can feel what each other is experiencing?"

Hades couldn't wait to find out. But for now, he settled for a kiss that hopefully expressed just part of what he felt in his heart. His mate had gone through a rotten day, he needed to eat and then the pair of them needed to get the hell out of the Underworld for a while.

Chapter Nineteen

"Hi honey, I'm home," Ali yelled as he rapped on the door to Claude and Sei's apartment loudly before opening it. "Please tell me you're decent 'cos we're coming in."

"Uncle Ali, Uncle Ali." Athena came running across the living room, her arms outstretched. Tony toddled along a little slower behind her.

"Oomph, you're getting big, princess," Ali teased as he caught her and swept her into a hug. "Have you got a big hello for Uncle Hades too?"

"Hi, Uncle Hades." Athena peered over Ali's shoulder, uncharacteristically shy. "You're like my Daddy."

Ali noticed Hades standing there, almost as if he wasn't sure what to do with himself. "Here, this is your daddy's brother," he said, offloading Athena into Hades' arms. "I've got to give this guy a hug too. Tony, my little man, how you doing?"

Bending over, he grabbed the toddler under the arms and hoisted him up.

"My goodness, you're another one that's put on ten pounds since I saw you last. When was that? Huh? A week ago?"

Tony chuckled, a delightful sound that Ali amplified by tickling a bare strip of belly fat. He was stouter than his sister, and rarely said anything, probably because Athena did the talking for both of them. But Ali had taken a shining to both toddlers. They gave the best hugs.

"Ali, you're back." Claude came striding into the living room, wearing his signature smile. "I thought Hades would have tucked you away in his mansion down there, and never let you see the light of day again."

"My mate's not like that," Ali said hotly, looking back over his shoulder to see Hades juggling Claude's daughter in his arms. She was whispering in his ear, goodness knows what because that girl had a vivid imagination, but the look of panic on Hades' face had reduced slightly.

Leaving the two together, and still holding Tony, Ali sidled closer to Claude. "That's a pretty snazzy tattoo you're sporting on your neck. Are you happy?" Claude demanded the moment he was out of Hades' earshot.

"Ecstatically so." Ali nodded. "Hades is a good man. I thought you knew that."

"I don't know him that well." Claude looked over. Hades' expression was still serious but Athena either didn't notice or didn't care. "He's never been up here."

"Oh." Ali was puzzled. Then he clicked. "Ooooh, he's only been down in the club. So, I'd better not take my man down there or he's going to be swarmed by lust drunk subs. My man's got serious power levels that would be like a drug to that lot. Damn, I was hoping we could have dinner here."

"And you still can." Draping his arm over Ali's shoulder, Claude led him to the huge couch. "Sei won't be long. He just needed to get his flippers wet.

You can have dinner with us. Now, tell me about the Underworld. Is it as freaky as I imagine it is?"

"What's freaky about it? Sure, it's run by demons, and the hellhounds are cute if you're a fan of drool. The furies are scary, but I only saw them today, and really, it's just like anywhere else that never sees the sun, and has a huge hellfire pit in the middle of it."

"Not like downtown Tulsa then." Claude shook his head. Looking over at Hades, he said, "Come and sit down, Hades. Athena will bend your ear off if you let her, and you don't look comfortable."

"I don't see non-demon children as a rule, and even the demon children tend to keep their distance from me." Hades' voice was so quiet, Ali knew he was feeling awkward. Holding Tony firmly with one arm, he patted the space beside him on the couch.

"Come and sit with me, babe. I blame Claude for all this," Ali said firmly. "The twins are how old now? And they don't know their uncle? Look,

Tony, this is your Uncle Hades." He poked the little boy in the belly and made him chuckle again. "He's a big bad freaky guy if you annoy him, but he's got the kindest heart. He's your Poppa's brother you know."

Tony gurgled, and drooled. Claude winced and pulled a handkerchief out of his pocket, leaning over to wipe his son's mouth. "Tony's teething," he said with a grimace. "I've got more shirts covered with drool than I ever had when I was single. How about I take these two off your hands, and get them ready for bed. By the time I'm finished, Sei will be here and we can eat."

Ali smirked. "He's still avoiding bath times then?"

"Every chance he gets," Claude sighed. "Come on babies," he got up, leaning over and grabbing Tony with one hand while he held out his other hand for Athena. With a child hanging from each hand like monkeys, he disappeared down the hallway.

Silence. Ali could still feel Hades' discomfort through their bond.

"Claude invited us to stay for dinner, but we don't have to stay," Ali whispered, knowing Claude had sharp ears. "I can just grab my phone and clothes and we can go back to my apartment."

"It's okay," Hades' smile was barely there. "I'm just not usually involved in any of my family's daily life. Meeting children, being in their private space. Most people go out of their way to avoid me."

Ali looked down the hallway and then back at his mate. "I don't think Claude's like that, and Sei did invite you to be his best man at his wedding. Maybe some people just think you wouldn't be interested in just hanging out."

"What do people even talk about when they just hang out?"

Realizing Hades was serious, Ali gave it some thought. "It would be different depending on who you were talking to. Like with Claude and Sei, I'd ask them about the twins, how the club is doing and topics like that. With other people, they might enjoy sports, or food for example, so we'd talk about that instead. It depends on people's interests."

The furrow between Hades' eyes deepened. "These interests. I suppose this hanging out would involve me being interested in those things to?"

"Not all the time." Ali shook his head, and then leaned on his mate's shoulder. "Like, I never thought about having kids, but I'll listen to Claude go on about how proud he is they are sleeping through the night. Sei is the worst. He just about busts his britches every time Tony takes a step and he's forever going on about how smart Athena is. Genius children, he calls them."

"The demon children all adore you and it appears Sei's offspring do to. Did you want kids?" Hades' tone didn't indicate if he cared either way. Ali decided to be honest.

"No, and not because of who you are either," he added quickly. "I've never really seen myself having kids. I grew up in a scurry that insisted their offspring followed a certain set of rules and if you didn't you were shunned for it. Even if my kids never saw their family on my side of things, I'd still know they were out there, disapproving, looking down their snotty noses at our adorable kiddies. I'd rather spend my time loving on you."

Hades didn't look convinced. Ali snuggled closer. "We still haven't talked about what happened with your uncle," Hades said slowly. "But with regards to having children, I wouldn't push the Fates to allow that for me. I got my dream mate. I wouldn't ask for anything else, although..." he trailed off. "You're not descended from a god line, are you?"

"Me?" Ali burst out laughing. "My family might act like their shit don't stink, but no, there's no godly genetics in my family tree. Oh, I'm so sorry," he slapped his hand over his mouth. "That means you'll never have kids, now you've claimed me."

Okay, that came out muffled from behind his hand, but Hades heard and if the smile and a warmth through their bond was anything to go by, Hades was pleased children wouldn't be in their future. The brush of lips Ali felt in his hair confirmed it. He would've said more, he would've turned up his face and got those lips brushing against something else, but with a rush of sea spray and the smell of seaweed, Poseidon arrived. *Good. I've got a bone to pick with you.*

/~/~/~/~/

Ali waited until they were halfway through dinner. Poseidon was joking and teasing his brother, increasing Ali's ire. Hades didn't seem to know what to say to get his brother off his back, and Ali didn't want to interfere because he didn't want to upset Claude. During a blessed lull, as Hades and Poseidon were both chewing on their steaks, Ali pounced.

"So, Sei, you were around when the realms were divided up. Who made the rule that said Hades has to allow each severely twisted soul to speak before he's sentenced in the Underworld?"

Hades grimaced, but the look was fleeing. "Sweetness," and Ali heard the warning tone.

"No, I want to know." Ali fixed Poseidon with a glare. "What do you do when you're communing with the fishes, huh? Swim around, play with your kraken, just to get out of bath times?"

"Gods are no longer allowed to interfere in the affairs of mortals," Poseidon sniffed. "I find the water soothing and as I'm part mer, I need to swim once in a while."

"But no heavy duty stuff, right?" Ali pointed his fork in Sei's direction. "I imagine Zeus is much the same, swaggering about in Olympus, getting fed grapes by nubile beauties and avoiding mortals like they were a plague."

"Zeus keeps in touch with mortal affairs through the use of computers." Poseidon grinned. "But yep, there's probably a bit of grape eating and swaggering involved."

There were times when Ali thought Sei was like Teflon. Everything slid off him, but he wouldn't be dissuaded by a sexy smile. "Why is it, if you can enjoy your realm for pleasurable purposes, and Zeus never strays from Olympus because he's worried his soul will be mated to a mortal, that Hades is the one out of all of you three who is doing all the work."

"There's no need for the ancient gods to do much anymore," Claude said quietly, exchanging a quick look with his mate. "People don't believe in them, and as Sei said, they aren't allowed to meddle in mortal affairs."

"That's the point I'm trying to make. If gods can't meddle in mortal affairs while they are living, then why does a god have to have anything to do with mortal souls when they're dead?"

Hades groaned, as if in protest, but Ali kept pushing. "Do you know how we spent this morning while you were loving on each other and your kids, doing the normal day to day shit that you do? We spent the morning and half the afternoon allowing almost one thousand damned souls their right to speech; them trying to justify their evil existence in the hopes they can either make a deal and work with the devil, or to try and commute their sentence. One of those asshole souls we saw today was my uncle for fart's sake, trying to get a cushy job in the Underworld while he waited for a chance at reincarnation that will never come because he was a shit during his lifetime."

"Oh, shit, your uncle? Ali, are you all right?" It was sweet Claude would worry, but his uncle was the last thing Ali was worried about.

"I'm fine, but it's my mate I'm worried about." Dropping his fork, Ali rested his hand on his mate's arm. "Day in, day out. Same shit, different shirt. What was it, Hades? Roughly fifteen hundred souls a week, and that's just the super bad souls that don't fit into the standard punishments. And Hades has to listen to them all. Why?"

Crickets. If they hadn't been in Claude and Sei's comfortable dinning room, Ali would have heard crickets. "You can't tell me, can you," he continued angrily. "Maybe whoever came up with the don't interfere rule, should've extended it after death. I read the news. I know how bad things are getting among the humans at least. And every one of those shits that shoots up a mall, or tries to wipe out an entire race of people ends up in Hades' realm. How would you like it if you had to sit there listening to crimes that make your hair curl, and then the asshole's justification for his behavior afterwards?"

"Sweetness, I told you, you don't have to attend the court days if they are going to bother you so much."

Hades was trying to be reasonable. Ali was well past that point and sliding straight towards enraged. "It's not about what I have to sit through. What about you? Doesn't anyone give a shit that you spend hours, huge hours working your domain every single freaking week, while they sit around playing happy families. It's not fair. It's not right. If they don't have to do anything but enjoy their realms, then why can't you be offered the same courtesy? Well?" Ali's glare was purely for Sei's benefit.

Poseidon pushed his plate away from him. "I regret, young chipmunk, I have no answers for you. We, and by we, I mean the gods and I, have always just stuck by what we've always done. I'm not saying we can't change. Look at me. But Hades has never once complained...."

"Who would listen to me?" Ali jumped as Hades slammed his fists on the table, jumped to his feet, and roared.

/~/~/~/~/

As Hades listened to his sweet mate defend and try and help him, an eon's worth of bitterness raged up inside of him. There probably wasn't an ancient god in existence who could claim to have a happy childhood and he was no exception. But when he'd been handed the mantle for the Underworld, he never imagined it would cut him off from everyone else.

For almost his entire existence, Hades had suffered on the fringe of life as everyone else knew it, weighed down by the sins of others and never shaking himself free. Until a sweet little chipmunk came along and showed him where the light was.

"Who would ever listen to me, if I did complain?" He yelled again, aware his power was pushing out from him like a tidal wave, but there was nothing he could do to stop it. "My family shunned me, turning away anytime I came near, unwilling to have anything to do with the man who deals with the scum life has to offer. How soon was it before I was tarred with the evil I have to deal with every day? Answer me, damn it."

"Hades, bro, you've got every reason to be upset," Poseidon got to his feet, eyeing him warily. "If we did anything wrong, then tell me now, so we can fix it, but I can't have you threatening my family."

"Threatening your family? Is that what you think I'm doing? By standing here? That's a fucking laugh.

You didn't even tell me when the twins were born, or when you were claimed by Claude. But I still cared about you and yours. I've never been a threat to anyone except those souls that deserve it. But you, you stand there all aquiver with salt spray in your veins and think I'm a threat. When I've never hurt you, never done you wrong. How do you think that makes me feel?"

"Hades is right, babe," Claude said, tugging on Poseidon's arm. "He's angry, and from the sounds of things he's got every right to be, but my wolf scents no danger from him. Sit down."

"I will not apologize for the way I feel, but if I've breached some social rule I don't know about, then to Claude I will say I'm sorry," Hades breathed roughly through his mouth. "But I haven't had a chance to know how to behave in polite company, have I? I spent eternity with a woman who wouldn't let me touch her, and why? Because no one would accept her either after she weaseled her way into her position and claimed a throne next to mine. That was the only worth I was to her. But even she got a break. She could go up to Olympus and spend time with her family, leaving me alone, still slogging at the job I've held since the Titans. I hate it, don't you get it? I always have, but what was the point of complaining? Was anyone going to help me out?"

"I will." Pushing back his chair, Ali wiped his mouth with his napkin, and laid it on the table before running his hand over Hades' fist. Hades had to unclench it. He needed Ali's touch more than he needed to breathe. "If the god of the sea and the almighty Zeus can't give a fuck, then I will. If you three rulers can't see that there need to be changes, then we'll make them anyway and to hell with the lot of you. Keeping things the way they've always been isn't a good enough excuse anymore. My mate is hurting, and that hurts me because I know he's been coping with his pain alone eons before I was born. You're not alone anymore, babe."

"I know," Hades felt his anger disappear under Ali's hand. "And I will praise the Fates from here to eternity for their gift. But think about it Sei. You complained for centuries how the non-interference law hurt your realm and there was nothing you could do. Do you still feel it? That anguish every time an oil tanker loses its cargo and pollutes your precious seas?"

Poseidon nodded, his face white. He reached for Claude blindly and Claude held him. "Imagine what it is like then," Hades said, "when you feel that pain over and over. Every time someone turns their back on you, or shudders as you walk by. Imagine the bleakness blanketing the core of your inner being, that you feel when your realm is polluted. Now imagine it twenty thousand times worse, because I feel like that every time I have to listen to an entitled soul who lies rather than face the consequences of their actions. Every single week they are dragged into my hall, spouting their lies, the darkness of their souls dragging me down with them. Every week, without fail, the numbers growing more and more as time goes on. It never stops."

Hades took a deep breath, letting it out slowly. "Brother, I was just like you, remember? I was raised in the sun. Now I live in a world that has no light. No light at all, until the Fates blessed me with Ali."

He gave Ali's hand a squeeze. "But there'll be no party to celebrate my mating, will there? No one in the family has bothered to offer me congratulations now this sweet soul wears my mark and I wear his. He's the only one who can bear to look at my face with sweetness in his expression, he's the only one who actively seeks my touch rather than shun me. I might be surrounded by evil, but my job is to keep that evil from tainting the world any more than it has. The price for that job, is that everyone around me sees me infected with that same evil, all except Ali, and your Athena who couldn't understand why she hadn't met me before your wedding and why

I didn't come around for meals more often." Hades' laugh was hollow. "Even you believed I was a threat to your family and your precious pack. I stood by you when you married Claude. It was a shame you couldn't do anything but try and belittle me in front of my mate in our first social outing since our mating. Some brother you turned out to be."

Looking down at his mate, Hades was pleased to see Ali smiling. "Are you ready? Think of your apartment and we'll be there. Claude, thank you for welcoming me into your home. Good-bye."

Picking up on Ali's thoughts, Hades translocated them. He didn't notice their surroundings; all he could see was his mate and even that image was blurry. Leaning against the wall and hugging his mate close, Hades broke down and cried for all that his life might have been.

Chapter Twenty

Ali woke up with a smile, covered in oil and dried come and a definite twinge in his ass. A half-used bottle of oil sat on the bedside table next to him, and the smell of sex mixed pleasantly with the almonds from the oil. *My precious mate does appreciate the joys of a good massage,* he thought as he wriggled around to watch Hades sleeping.

Relaxed, Hades still managed to retain the godly aspects of his personality. But with his long black lashes resting on his high cheek bones, and his wide pink lips opened slightly as he snored, Ali didn't think he'd ever seen anyone so beautiful. Hades had sprawled out as he slept, his naked body making a fine display against Ali's dark blue sheets.

I'll get him some food, Ali thought fondly as he wriggled gingerly over the other side of the bed. After the outburst the night before, his mate needed his sleep and Ali would jump on anyone who dared disturb him. He noticed a message orb sitting on the bathroom counter as he went through and turned on the shower. *That means you too, Folsom.*

Fifteen minutes later, Ali sauntered into the kitchen, wearing a pair of briefs and not much else. *I seriously need to do some laundry,* he thought as he opened up the refrigerator door. Picking up a packet of bacon, he sniffed at it, and grimaced. *We need groceries too. I wonder....*

Turning, Ali spotted a small pile of clothes on his kitchen counter – his wallet, phone and keys resting on top of them, and his shoes placed neatly on the floor. "The god of the sea is useful for something then," he muttered, checking his phone. It was dead, so Ali plugged it into its charger, and checked his wallet. His money and cards were still all there, although Ali didn't expect anything less. Claude would have a major furry fit if anyone dared steal from him.

Unwilling to wake up his mate, Ali scribbled a quick note on his pad by his computer, and threw on the clothes he'd worn to the wedding. *A bit posh for the corner store,* he giggled to himself. Sliding into his shoes, he grabbed his wallet, stuffed it in his pocket and headed for the door.

Opening it, he was stunned to see a man who bore a definite family resemblance to him, his arm up as if ready to knock. It took him a moment to realize who it was.

"Larry, what are you doing here?" He hissed, casting a quick glance down the hall to the bedroom, before focusing back on his cousin again. "You'll be shunned by the scurry if anyone knows you've come here."

"Your father told me to come and get you. You haven't been answering your phone." Larry twisted his hand, hopping on one foot and then the other.

"Father?" Ali was shocked. Stepping back from the door, he indicated inside. "You'd better come in."

"I can't stay," Larry said even as he darted in the door, looking around as though he expected to walk into a brothel or something similar. "Your father said to come and get you. Aunt Lucy's dead and this morning Uncle Thorn's body was found at a…."

Collapsing in a chair, Larry covered his face with his hands. "It's so awful," he moaned, dropping his hands into his lap. There were tears in his eyes. Ali remembered that while he hadn't followed Uncle Thorn's teachings, Larry had been a willing pupil. "There's going to be a huge scandal. People are calling uncle's phone all over the place, demanding to know where their merchandise is, and no one knows what they're talking about. The police are sticking their nose into scurry business, and your father's worried sick the papers will get hold of the news. Our name will be plastered all over the country. It'll be a scandal."

Moving slowly over to another chair, Ali sat down, working hard to make sure none of his emotions were showing on his face. "Are you trying to tell me, you and father are upset because of a possible scandal over Thorn's death? What about Lucy?"

"What about her?" Larry seemed confused at the questions. "Uncle said she died, falling down some stairs. She broke her neck. There wasn't time for her to shift or anything. Uncle came by, maybe a week ago and said he had something to do, but that he'd handle all the funeral arrangements. Then he disappears, and no one hears anything from him until the police start banging on the door this morning. Apparently, he's been dead for days."

What the…? I only saw him yesterday. But then the rest of what Larry said sunk in. It was possible Thorn could've been dead at least a week. *Clearly souls don't care if their remains are found or not.*

"Where did they find his body?" Ali remembered the sharp suit his dead uncle arrived at the Underworld in.

"An apartment," Larry wailed. "It was registered in the name of some woman none of us have ever heard of. The police said there were drugs there, and food, and all sorts of kinky toys around, like someone was trying to frame Uncle for something or wreck his reputation. If the papers find out, our family name will be destroyed."

When they find out what Uncle Thorn had been up to in life, the family name will be the least of their problems. Ali leaned back in his chair. "That still doesn't tell me why my father wants to see me. I haven't been allowed to go near anyone in the scurry for decades. I had nothing to do with Thorn's death or Lucy's and I have no contacts in the police department. What does he expect me to do?"

Larry looked over his left shoulder, and then his right, before leaning forward, resting his elbows on his knees. "He wants you to talk to the pack alpha," he whispered.

"Claude?" Now Ali was even more puzzled. "Claude hasn't got anything to do with this either. He runs his club, and looks after his family and friends, that's it. The scurry is nowhere near pack territory. It's got nothing to do with him."

"No, no, we're not suggesting he's got anything to do with it." Ali could smell Larry's fear and that didn't surprise him. For all their snobby ways, no one in the scurry would take on a wolf, especially an alpha. "Your father just thought, maybe you could have a word to him, on the quiet, and see if he can...."

"See if he can do what exactly?" Ali could feel his anger rising. "Tell the police to back off, stop investigating the shit Uncle Thorn got up to in his life, in the hopes all this will just be swept under the carpet and no one will know about it? You don't need Claude to do that. You can just call the shifter council and get them to liaise with the police."

"No. No. We can't." The smell of fear got stronger and Larry was twisting his hands so hard, Ali thought he'd pull off a finger. "Uncle Thorn... Your father's been through some of his papers and... there might have been a few things...."

Ali remembered what Folsom had read out the day before. "Evidence of human trafficking you mean. Keeping slaves. Murdering his bond mate. Those kinds of things?"

"What?" Larry sounded suitably outraged, but Ali could smell the deceit rising in the air. "How can you say such things about a family member. There're just some irregularities in Uncle's accounts that's all. Your father thought you could help with them, see where he was getting all his money from."

"I know where Uncle Thorn got his money from." Ali smiled as his mate's power filled the living room. "Larry, meet my fated mate, Hades, Ancient Greek God and Lord of the Underworld. In the course of helping my mate with his duties, well, let's just say I have seen our dearly departed Uncle a little more recently than you have. I know exactly what he's been up to."

Larry's face went paper white, and he clutched his throat, swallowing hard. His eyelids fluttered shut and then he slumped into a dead faint, still sitting on the chair.

Looking over his shoulder, Ali grinned at his mate. "Morning, sweetheart. If you have that sort of effect on my cousin, I can't wait for you to meet my mom and dad. Fancy some breakfast?"

Chapter Twenty One

The last thing Hades expected when he woke up in Ali's bed that morning, was to be crammed into a car far too small for his tall frame, with an unconscious guy in the back seat who bore a startling resemblance to Ali. He'd been showering, pondering the message he'd gotten from Folsom that morning about Cerberus, when he heard a yell coming from the living room.

A quick click of his fingers had him dried and dressed in no time, but as he strode into the living room, determined to eviscerate anyone who was upsetting his mate, he was shocked to see Ali smiling. When the cousin, Larry, still hadn't woken up ten minutes later after his faint, Ali suggested they have a quick bite to eat, and then they would take Larry home. Fortunately, Hades' clicking powers worked on food too, as Ali didn't have a lot in his cupboards.

"Have you ever thought about getting a bigger car?" Hades tried to get his legs in a more comfortable position under the dashboard. "Money would never be an issue for you anymore, and… and…." It wasn't as though he objected to being in a car, exactly, but he thought he might be less worried about becoming road kill if the car was a bit bigger, didn't have doors that rattled, or an exhaust system that sounded as though it was about to come off.

"Aw, babe." Ali smirked, reaching over and patting Hades' knee. *Keep your hands on the damn wheel.* "I've been driving for decades, and this little car might look rough, but it's always started first time every time."

Hades cringed as a car swerved in front of them, nearly pushing them off the road. Ali tooted his horn, but kept on going. It was time to try a different tactic. "Sweetness, you said you were going to introduce me to your parents."

"Yep. Well, mom and dad, and I imagine there will be a few uncles and aunties there as well. If news about Thorn has spread, I know my dad will have called for reinforcements. We have to keep up the family name and that means showing unity to all outsiders," he added in a snottier voice than Hades was used to. "That's what my dad says," he added. "The family name is the only thing that matters in that scurry."

"Well, if your father sets a great store about appearances, wouldn't it be better if we arrived in a style befitting a god?" Hades suggested.

"You mean like your four horses and that gorgeous carriage?" Ali laughed as he steered the car into a quiet upmarket neighborhood. "I'm not sure they'd settle enough to get us anywhere with all the cars around."

"A limo, maybe?" Hades was getting desperate. He wasn't sure if they went much further his legs would be able to unfold enough to get out, not to mention what driving in a small car was doing to his nerves. "That's what you call it, isn't it? Those fancy long cars, that celebrities ride around in and people with money?"

Sighing, Ali pulled over to the side of the road. They hadn't parked by one of the giant gates Hades could see, so clearly, they hadn't reached their destination yet. Turning off the engine, Ali swiveled in his seat. "Babe, what is it you have against my car?"

Hades looked at his knees, then back at his mate. "Isn't it obvious? It's not that I have anything against your car specifically," he added quickly, "I just think you need to be thinking about your new status as my mate too."

"I suppose I should be grateful you even got in the thing," Ali grumbled. "Claude's Hummer is far bigger than this and Poseidon was terrified of getting in it. Apparently, he'd never been in a car before then."

Hades sympathized with his brother. He knew exactly how the God of the Sea felt. "I'm sure you're a good driver," *We haven't crashed yet,* "But I think making a decisive statement, when visiting your parents for the first time in decades, would help set the tone for the meeting, don't you?"

"Honey, that meeting's going to be a crap-fest anyway." Ali shook his head. "But fine, you can change this car into a limo if you want, although usually a limo comes with a driver. And, I'm not using a limo for everyday transport, okay? I might, just might, agree to a slightly larger and more powerful Hummer than Claude has got, just because I want to show off how amazing my mate is, but nothing else, okay? I am not with you for your gems, gold, goodness knows what else you have and your fancy mansions. I'm with you because you're mine."

"I'll give Folsom a treat and he can drive for us." Hades felt the relief as he worked his magic. His legs finally had room to move. Folsom was sitting in the front of the limo, a dark chauffeur cap on his head. The demon turned in his seat, his eyes sparkling. In his human form, he was quite a pleasant young man.

"My lord, my lord, what a huge surprise." Folsom grinned, showing perfect white teeth. "Does this mean…?"

"No shopping malls yet, Folsom," Hades warned. "We're visiting Ali's parents and they're not likely to be pleasant. If, and I mean it, if you behave yourself as a respectable representative of the Underworld while we're there, then I will allow you to take us to a mall for one hour, while you shop. But that's only if not one thing gets singed, or blown up while we're at Ali's parents."

"But what if it's not my fault," Folsom pleaded. "What if you or the consort are in danger?"

"Just behave yourself, Folsom. I'll protect my consort. Now drive. You do know how to drive don't you?"

"Ooh, yes." Folsom squealed as he turned the key in the ignition. "There was this one time, only a few years ago, when I came up here with Mischa. Well, he had a thing about sports cars…."

Tuning out Folsom's story, Hades focused on Ali. He was leaning back looking out of the smoked glass windows, but he must have sensed Hades' gaze, because he turned his head and smiled.

"Do those long legs of yours feel better now?"

"Thank you, yes," *and my nerves,* although Hades didn't say that. Instead he slid across the seat, wrapping his arm around Ali's shoulder. "And thank you for being so understanding." Hades didn't think he'd ever get tired of the warm glow that flowed through him when his mate snuggled into him.

"I've been thinking about what you said," Ali sighed. "About appearances and things like that. It's all my parents ever cared about. Silly things, like clothes. They had to come from an upmarket brand, or better yet, from a designer. I don't think my dad owns a pair of off the rack jeans, or pants, and my mother is never seen without pearls dangling around her neck. It's ridiculous. Our animals live in the forest areas, but they barely go out past their manicured lawns."

Glancing out the window, Hade saw the limo had turned into a long, long driveway and sure enough, not one blade of grass stood out from the regimented cut. "Where do your parents shift then, if that's not a rude question?" Hade could see some low bushes and a mass of roses, but he wasn't sure a chipmunk would appreciate the thorns in their fur.

Ali stuck his nose in the air. "If one cannot resist the pushiness of one tiny furry creature, one must ensure they confine their furry form to the conservatory at the rear of the property," he said in a voice so unlike his own, Hades knew he must be imitating his mother.

"I was the only one who broke the rules," Ali continued in his normal tone. "I would drive to the nearest forest, leave my clothes in the car, and shift. I could be out there all day sometimes. My parents hated it. My mother would sniff and turn her nose up when I got home, as though the smell of dirt was offensive to her. Father would mumble something about damn savages and disappear into his study."

"I'll buy you a forest," Hade promised. "One on every continent if you desire, so you can try them all out for yourself."

"You don't have to do that," Ali laughed as he snuggled in closer. "But I was thinking, maybe a suit might be more appropriate for today. Your reputation is important to me."

"I was thinking maybe another kilt was more in keeping with your sparkling personality." Hades adored watching the way the tartan swung with every sway of Ali's hips. "Something like you wore for court day, what do you think?"

"My parents will hate it, which means I love it."

Ali's peels of laughter were loud over the crunch of tires on gravel. Folsom was bringing the car to a halt in front of a reasonably impressive house. Just looking at it, Hades felt a shiver run down his spine. The Garcia mansion appeared colder and more lifeless than his own mansion in the Underworld which was saying something.

When Folsom jumped out, ready to get the door, Hades clicked his fingers and smiled at the sassy outfit Ali was in. The kilt was green and gold this time, that contrasted perfectly with Ali's curls. Combined with a matching green top, his black boots and black leather coat that mirrored Hades' own, Hades thought he looked adorable.

They climbed out of the car, Hades resting his hand on Ali's lower back. "How are we going to get Larry inside?" Ali asked.

"Folsom can bring him, can't you Folsom?" Hades said firmly. "And make sure you announce us fully, when the door is answered."

"On it, my Lord." Folsom leaned over the back seat of the limo, dragging the comatose Larry into his arms and then over one shoulder. "Ooh, do you think I should put on a British accent like all those fancy butlers have?"

"Don't over do it." Hades was more worried about how still Ali was. "Are you okay?"

"It's been a long time since I've been here." Inhaling sharply, Ali shook out his hands as he let the breath out. "Let's do this."

Chapter Twenty Two

Walking up the steps behind Folsom, Ali tried not to let his nerves show. Just coming through the gates, he felt the weight of his parents' disappointment dragging on his shoulders, making him feel like a teenager all over again. *I am better than this,* he told himself firmly. *I've built a good life for myself, and the Fates thought I was good enough to be a mate for a god. There is nothing my parents can say or do that can hurt me now.*

Hades' presence was like a strong wall beside him. Folsom knocked sharply on the door, and after a brief minute it was opened. Ali didn't recognize the face of the man who answered, but then a lot would have happened in eighty years.

"If you would be so kind as to inform the owners of the house that Hades and Ali, Lords of the Underworld have arrived," Folsom said with a lofty tone. "Also, I believe this is yours." He dumped Larry on the doorstep and turned back towards the car.

Wrinkled eyes looked confused. "The Lord of Underworld? Oh, my stars, is this about Master Thorn? Yes, yes, come in. I'll let the Master and the Lady of the House know you are here immediately."

"He doesn't even know who you are?" Hades whispered as they stepped into the Grand Foyer.

"I didn't recognize him, but then that's not surprising. It has been a while." A very long while. Ali looked around. Some things, like the height of the ceilings, and the sweeping staircase that led to the household's private quarters would never change. Everything else, from the royal red carpet to the gold vases holding masses of flowers were so new Ali wanted to look for price tags. The black coverings on two large oval mirrors were also a new look for the entrance hall.

Ali nudged his mate. "I'll bet these are the only mirrors covered apart from the one in the drawing room, which is where we'll be asked to go.

Appearances are everything in this house, but only in public spaces."

Just then the butler came back in. "The Master and the Lady of the house are in deep mourning, but the Lady has graciously agreed to see you this one time without an appointment."

"Appointment?" Hades' single growl bounced around the marble.

"What my consort meant," Ali said quickly, as the butler's face paled. Hades certainly had that effect on people. "What he meant is that we didn't realize we needed an appointment for a family matter. We only returned my cousin Larry because it was clear he was unable to return to the house on his own. I was under the impression my father wished to speak to me, and had sent my cousin to let me know of his wishes. But if we've come at a deeply troubling time, please let your Master know he can make an appointment to speak to us when we're free. As you can appreciate, my consort is an extremely busy god, and this morning's outing has inconvenienced us to no small degree."

"Er.. er… er…. You're the Master's son Mister Larry was meant to fetch to the house?" The butler put his hand out to prevent himself from falling. Fortunately, he was near the door frame.

"In the flesh," Ali showed all his teeth. "But it's fine, you not knowing me and all. I have been banished from the scurry for many years. Please convey our message to the Master of the house and we'll be on our way. Good day."

He managed a slight nod, and turned towards the door, his mate hard by his side. *3… 2… 1….* "Ali, is that you?" Ali turned at the sound of his mother's voice. "I can't believe it, as I live and breathe. My son has come home in our hour of need. You may kiss me."

She held out her hand, her other hand busy dabbing non-existent tears from her immaculate face. Miranda Garcia hadn't changed since Ali saw her last, beyond a tightening in her cheeks and under her neck. Hades was looking at her hand as though it would poison him, and Ali wouldn't put his mother past it when it came to him at least.

Ignoring the offer, he rested his hand on his mate's arm, and plastered on another fake smile. "Mrs. Garcia, my apologies on intruding on your grief. Larry fainted and we had no choice but to bring him here," he waved at Larry who was slowly stirring on a couch not big enough for a human body. "We were just leaving. It was never our intention to intrude. My mate is a busy a man."

"Your mate, yes." Ali knew Miranda hadn't missed a detail of Hades' clothing or his power which seeped from him even when he was calm. Her quick perusal of him was a lot more dismissive. "You never mentioned you had been claimed Aloysius. I imagine congratulations are in order, of course. Perhaps, your exalted mate could join us. His arrival at this moment is indeed fortuitous and must be an intervention from the

Fates themselves. We've been bereft since we learned of poor Thorn's untimely death."

She shot a scathing look at the butler who was still leaning on the door frame. "It will be more private in the drawing room. When the staff have recovered themselves, perhaps they can serve light refreshments. Shall we?"

Ali risked a quick glance at Hades as they followed Miranda through a reception room and then through French doors to the drawing room. Ali hadn't spent much time there as a child. The room was strictly for visitors and was furnished accordingly. The gilt around the fireplace was new, and the wallpaper didn't have a mark on it. The chairs were designed for intimidation rather than comfort and Ali longed for his throne chair as he perched on the closest one.

Hades, for reasons of his own, stayed standing, a brooding hunk of menace that had Ali's blood boiling despite the circumstances, his hand resting lightly on the back of the chair Ali had taken. Miranda arranged herself in what Ali had always considered "her" chair. High backed, with winged sides, the upholstery was a deep velvet blue which highlighted Miranda's pale skin and hair.

"Hades, may I call you Hades? Of course, it must be fine; we are family after all. Hades, I must implore you. Something must be done about my husband's uncle's death. Thorndike Garcia. Perhaps you've heard of him?" She peered up at Hades, a picture of innocence, and yet Ali could see the calculations in her eyes.

"The correct way to address an ancient God is 'my Lord,'" Hades said brusquely. "You're forgiven this time, as it is unlikely you've crossed paths with anyone of my exalted lineage before, but such a slight won't go unpunished in future."

Ali twisted his whole upper body to openly stare at his mate. A brief meeting of eyes, Ali winked and turned back again to see a splash of red blooming over Miranda's cheeks.

"My lord, yes of course, if you insist. We have just met. One would hope, as you get to know us better, more familiarity might be allowed." Miranda had lost her strident tone. "But please, in the name of the relationship we have with your... partner," she couldn't hide her distaste, Ali thought gleefully, "Perhaps you could see your way clear to providing assistance with our beloved Thorn's untimely death."

A chill filled the air. Ali wanted to clap his hands in excitement, but he took a lesson from his mate and kept his face impassive.

"Twice you have insulted me," Hades' voice was low and full of menace. "I would suggest keeping our conversation to a minimum. What is it you expect me to do about Thorndike Garcia?"

Miranda's eyes widened. "I can't think for a second how I could have insulted you a second time, my Lord, but surely it is obvious our needs regarding dear Thorndike. He died far too young. He must be returned to his life, to handle his numerous affairs. The police, the FBI, even the shifter council are threatening investigations and he needs to be here to put paid to the nasty rumors going around about his life and the circumstances of his passing."

"You want me to go against the will of the Fates in regard to the mortal chipmunk shifter, Thorndike Garcia?"

"Er..." Miranda's eyes darted around the room. "No, I mean yes, I mean it's surely not a big deal to the Fates. You control the Underworld. You are the authority on death. Surely, you wouldn't miss one shifter?"

"I do rule the Underworld. It's my job to ensure that ruthless souls, blackened by their sins are not let loose on the earth again. Your request is denied."

Ali felt a hand on his shoulder, and he looked up. "We have places to be," Hades said simply.

Standing, Ali smoothed down his kilt. It really was beautifully soft material. "Mrs. Garcia...."

"You can't go!" Miranda was on her feet too. "You dare to imply our dear family member has blackened his soul somehow, and then you just up and leave? Arthur, Arthur," she called out as the door on the other side of the room opened and Ali watched his father stride through. "We have a god in the drawing room, an actual ancient god and he's refusing to do anything about Thorndike."

Arthur had aged since Ali had seen him last, as the shots of gray in his hair and the deepened lines on his face testified. Ali knew the moment his father spotted him as the lines across his forehead and around his mouth intensified.

"Aloysius, what on earth are you doing in that ridiculous outfit. Have you no respect for the dead?"

"If you're referring to Uncle Thorn, then no, I don't actually. But then I was present at his sentencing in Hades' court and he wasn't very respectful to me either." Ali reached for Hades' hand.

"Sentencing, what do you mean, sentencing? The man's dead. Found in very unfortunate circumstances. But there's never been any suggestion by anyone that he led anything but a blameless life. That's what I want to discuss with you. You must use your influence with that mangy wolf shifter to ensure any investigations into Thorn's affairs are stopped. The whole torrid affair threatens to destroy our family name."

"See what I mean?" Ali looked up at Hades sadly.

"The pits are definitely preferable to being here." Hades turned, so he was blocking Ali from seeing his parents, giving him his whole focus. *Such a sweet mate.* "What would you have me do, my sweetness? I can render this house to rubble and destroy all who live here. You could practice calling Juno and his friends – I'm sure they wouldn't object to a snack. A call to Poseidon would have him here in an instant, calling the waters and drowning all who malign *his* precious mate. I have to confess. I'm not sure on protocol here. What does one do to insulting people whose only positive thing they've ever done in their mundane lives was to provide the genetic material that resulted in you?"

"Are you deliberately ignoring us in our own home?"

Ali flinched. His father's voice was close, but Hades tucked him against his side, keeping his free hand fisted as he turned to face Ali's parents.

"One can only assume the only person in this household with a working brain and a clean soul is the man I have in my arms." Hades clipped out every word. "I don't have to have anything to do with you. I am a god and you are so far below my notice even a slug on the ground ranks higher in my esteem than you do."

Arthur gasped and Miranda gripped her pearl necklace. But Hades hadn't finished. "The moment you knew of my mating with your offspring, you sought to claim familiarity with me. I have no desire to have anything to do with you, so I won't. The next time you see me, and my darling immortal mate, we will be presiding at your sentencing in the one court no evil soul can escape. You will be on your knees before me, just as Thorn was, and no amount of lies from your mouth will mitigate the darkness in your soul."

"I haven't... I'd never...." Ali could smell the acrid scent of his parents' fear.

"The only decent thing you ever brought into the world is walking out of the door with me." Hades tilted his neck slightly as he viewed the shocked couple. "Hmm, maybe, if you spent the next hundred years doing good works, you might be spared meeting me again, Miranda. I'm not sure, but Fates know I have no wish to look upon either of your faces again. Rest assured, if I do, I will show no mercy and even the claims of blood ties to my beloved consort won't save you from your eternal torment. Good day."

Ali allowed himself to be swept along, his emotions in turmoil, the only solid thing in his life, guiding his steps. He was on the threshold of the drawing room, when Hades turned one more time. "And Arthur?" Miranda and Arthur were clutching each other and the tears on Miranda's face were real this time. *It's a shame they were never for me,* Ali thought as Hades curled his lip.

"Cooperate with the authorities, Arthur. If one more innocent person dies as the result of the operation you and Thorn were running, then Death himself will be instructed by the Fates to take you directly to the Underworld where the Furies themselves will determine your eternity. Miranda, it might be time to question your husband as to where the money for all your recent renovations came from. It's not too late for you if you live a long enough life filled with good works."

The Furies? But that means father has.... Ali's knees turned to water. Only Hades' strong hand stopped him falling to the floor. Scooping him up, Hades strode past the confused butler, and an equally baffled Larry, heading for the front door. "It is time for you to seek new employment, sir, along with the rest of the staff," Hades said to the butler in passing. To Larry he nodded. "That career you wanted in culinary school? I'd get on that today. You do not want to be caught up in the shit storm that will hit this household later today."

Fresh air. Ali couldn't get enough of it. Black spots shimmered in front of his eyes. He was struggling to breathe. Only vaguely aware of Hades holding him close as he moved towards the limo, Ali's eyelids fluttered, and he passed out.

Chapter Twenty Three

"My Lord," Folsom dashed forward as Hades strode down the steps of the Garcia household, Ali limp in his arms. "The Consort, Ali, is he all right? Do you need me to…."

"Burn this place to the ground?" Hades snarled as he carefully maneuvered himself into the back of the limo taking care not to hit Ali's head on the door. "It's very tempting. But the Fates will not approve and as they've been paying particular attention to me and my mate recently, I do not want to piss them off. Just drive. Find a mall. Do your shopping. I have to tend to my mate."

The passenger door was shut carefully once he was seated, but Hades barely noticed. He trailed his fingers down Ali's cute nose, across his cheeks, and ran his forefinger over Ali's lips. *Why did I do it?* He cursed himself. *Why did I have to mention the Furies in relation to Ali's father when my mate was standing right next to me?*

Truth be told, Hades' ability to see the darkness in a living individual's soul, and the extent of his sins wasn't usually an issue. There had been a few times during the course of his existence, when he'd used that ability to nudge a few souls towards a more positive direction in life. But today…. *I was angry,* Hades reasoned with himself. *Angry that Ali deserved so much better when it came to his family. Those stuck-up, no-good, dark-souled ingrates. Are their souls that blackened with hate they fail to see the beauty, honesty, and goodness of their son?*

"I think you're pretty terrific too, you know," Ali said sleepily.

Hades looked down. *My mate's okay.* "I'm so sorry," he said quickly. "I never meant for you to hear about your Father's sins like that."

"It's okay." Ali tried to sit up, but Hades gently held him in place.

"Just rest a moment. You've had a huge shock."

Ali's shoulders relaxed against Hades' legs. "I thought Uncle Thorn was bad enough," he whispered. "But then, I suppose, with the slavery charges... all those innocents?" He trailed off, his words lifting as a question.

"Young boys and girls," Hades said gravely. "I am honor bound not to interfere in mortal affairs, but as soon as I saw your father I knew."

"He has to be stopped."

Hades nodded. "I can't do anything. I can only hope with the authorities investigating Thorn's death...."

"They may not get it." Ali struggled to get up again and this time Hades let him. "My father is damn clever. There'll be other family members involved. What if, what if they hide the evidence, or worse, the bodies? Hades, what if they kill the evidence?"

It took everything in Hades' control not to react to the sheer panic in his mate's voice. He was honor bound to live by the one rule all gods abided by which meant he had to choose his words carefully. "It is a tragic situation. There's no proof. Authorities aren't able to see the stains on a person's soul the way I can. All gods are bound by the non-interference law. Let's say, for example, we went to my brother about this. *Poseidon* wouldn't be able to do anything either."

Hades held still under Ali's intense gaze. He was briefly aware the car had come to a stop. A slam of the driver's door let him know Folsom was off to wreak havoc on the psyche of the local mall staff. But Ali was his only focus. *Please, understand.*

A slight widening of Ali's eyes made the corner of Hades' lip curl upwards. "*You* can't do anything," Ali said softly. "Poseidon couldn't do anything to save those poor souls if I told him. But if I was having a talk with my good friend, Claude, like my father asked me to – you heard him. He was referring to Claude with his mangy wolf comment, then the non-interference laws haven't been broken, right?"

"I would never tell you who you could and couldn't talk to," Hades said as Ali's smile widened. "I'm sure that would be in breach of The Good Mates Guide."

"The Good Mates Guide. We must get one of them." Ali chuckled. Looking around, he said, "Why have we stopped? I need to get to Claude's club. Oh, shit, are we even welcome there anymore?"

Hades flushed as he remembered their last visit, and his subsequent outburst. "I'm sure when they realize the seriousness of the situation, they'll hear you out. But we do have to wait a few minutes. I did promise Folsom he could go shopping. Although...." Looking out the car window he saw Folsom running towards them, two burly security guards trying to catch him. "It seems like Folsom's knack of getting into trouble with humans works in our favor today. Brace yourself."

Folsom dived into the driver's seat, turning the key and peeling out of the parking lot like the hellhounds were after him. "That dumb shit," he yelled. "That pimple covered, no good, stuck up little... little... shit!"

"Don't tell me. They didn't have the shirt you liked in your size?" Hades asked calmly as he draped his arm over his mate's shoulder.

"It was the wrong damn color," Folsom cursed. "Honestly, is it too much to ask that the one time I get to go shopping in two fucking years, that they actually have the shirt I want in the right color. Have you seen the so-called new trends this year? Only one color suitable for my delectable skin tone. I mean, I ask you. Who's hiring the clothes designers these days?"

"We're going to Claude's. Try not to crash the car on the way."

"Crash the car, as if I would crash the car carrying my Lord and his consort," Folsom grumbled. "Stupid little git telling me 'oh, that's a very popular color this year. It can take up to ten days before we can have one delivered. They're in such high demand'. High demand, I ask you.

High demand? I just wanted one damn shirt."

"Is the store clerk able to continue his duties?" Hades was well aware how his PA could be.

"He might have a bit of a limp. They wouldn't even let me buy the clothes I'd already got picked out. They were sitting right there, on the counter. My Lord, can you...?"

"Get us to Claude's in one piece, and I'll see what I can do." Hades could feel Ali's shoulders shaking. Looking down he saw his mate had his hand over his mouth, his eyes shining above it. Hades shook his head slightly. It would not do for Folsom to think they were laughing at him. But after the events of the afternoon, Folsom's continued grumbling and cursing was a welcome relief.

/~/~/~/~/

The scent of salt spray alerted Hades to his brother's presence. Ali had been closeted with Claude for over half an hour, but in keeping with the non-interference laws, Hades chose to sit in the dance bar area. Given it was still late afternoon, the only other person there was a bartender and once Hades ordered a bottle of his favorite cognac and one glass, the man left him alone.

"I don't have to invite you to sit down in your mate's establishment," Hades said, tipping up his glass and taking a sip. "Or do you prefer to lurk these days."

Poseidon slid into the booth across from him. "I heard, or rather, Claude has shared some of what you two have been going through. I wondered if there was anything I could do to help?"

"With Ali's family?" Setting the glass on the table, Hades kept his hands around it as he eyed his brother cautiously. "You're as bound by the non-interference laws as I am."

"I wasn't referring to the Garcias. I meant you and Ali. This must have been rough on both of you, and you've not been together long."

Hades looked down at his glass. "Ali is the most resilient person I've ever come across. He adapts and goes with the flow no matter what life throws at him. While I don't doubt these circumstances might hit him hard sooner or later, I'll deal with any fallout when it comes."

"But what about you?" Sei insisted. "How are you coping with all this?"

"Me?" Sei's words were enough of a shock to have Hades glance up at his brother, a chuckle hovering in the back of his throat. "Since when have you cared about my mental health? I'm fine. I'm always fine. So long as I have Ali, I don't see that changing any time soon."

"Hades look." Sei made to reach over the table and then pulled back, resting his entwined fingers on the table. "My mate tells me I can be a bit thoughtless at times."

"Like the last time Ali and I visited."

"Like the last time you and Ali visited," Sei agreed. "I'm not saying he's right, although, you know, it's

Claude and he's pretty special and blunt enough to tell me what he thinks. But you see, just because I've always been a randy sod, and I know a lot of people think I don't see past the end of my dick, I am capable of genuine feelings."

"I'm sure you are." Hades wasn't sure what to make of Sei in his current "human" form. He preferred the God of the Sea look. With his almost white blond hair hanging in a plait down to his ass, and his unbelievably young features, Sei had such an innocent look about him, it'd be impossible for Hades to punch him.

"But see, the thing is," Sei hadn't finished. "I've always thought we've had a spot of the bro-code going on. You know. We don't talk about mushy stuff or share our feelings, but it's understood, like underneath, that we care about each other."

"Are you talking about between you and me, or are you including Zeus in this bro-code thing you think we have going on?" Hades had never heard that term used before, but he wasn't about to admit it.

"Zeus has lost touch with mortality," Sei scoffed. "I can't remember the last time he came down from that lofty throne of his and actually walked among real people. I figure humans were probably still living in log huts at the time. So, no, perhaps not him, although he is our brother too. But you and me. Especially recently. I thought we'd connected, that we were tight."

"Tight?" Hades lifted his glass and took another sip of his cognac. "Is that another modern reference I know nothing about?"

"Don't be such an arrogant shit," Sei glared. "You know what I'm talking about."

"Fine. We're tight." The cognac was settling in Hades' gut easier than the conversation. "If that's all you've got to say…."

"No, damn it, it isn't. Why didn't you tell me?"

Hades was confused. "Tell you what? Is this your oblique way of asking me if my outburst the other night had any truth to it?"

"I know you didn't lie. I want to know why I didn't know about what you were going through sooner. I could've done something."

The thing was, Hades could tell Sei was being completely open and honest. But it didn't change the fact that his desire to help was thousands of years too late.

"What would you have done?" Hades asked quietly. "When the other gods on Olympus shunned me, what could you have said or done that would've changed that? How would you have reacted if you saw members of our own family move away when I walked into a room. When Zeus gave Persephone free reign over my life and realm, without even talking to me about it, what could you have done? The centuries of loneliness I went through, even though I was supposedly married – would any of that have changed if you'd known? Or maybe, just maybe, you saw how I was treated, you knew how Persephone talked about me on her trips home, and you did nothing anyway."

"I genuinely didn't know. I thought you just liked being alone." Sei looked down at his hands. Hades felt a pang of something akin to sympathy, and caused a second glass to appear in his hand. Pouring Sei a shot, he pushed it across the table. For a while, the two men sipped in silence.

"I've been thinking about this a lot," Sei said suddenly, putting his glass on the table. "What pisses me off is I should've known what was happening to you. I remember those big parties Zeus liked to throw; everyone standing around gossiping about everyone else. I think back on it now, and I know you were there, at least in the early days, so why didn't I see anything going on?"

"Did you want to?" Hades asked bluntly. "Or, because I recall those parties too, were you too busy avoiding the people you had fucked, in favor of finding someone who wasn't intimately acquainted with your dick?"

Sei had been about to take a sip from his glass. He coughed, and then laughed. "I was such a horn dog back then," he said fondly.

"And you weren't any different to anyone else in Olympus," Hades sighed. "The thing is, as gods, we prided ourselves on facing all dangers with a laugh and a sword. Most of the gods were still being worshipped in those days, and the sheer arrogance that stemmed from that was incredible. No one talked about feelings."

Sei stopped laughing. "But you weren't worshipped."

"No, I wasn't." Hades held his brother's eyes. He had no need to look away.

"And you saw me, and everyone else…."

"As arrogant souls who wouldn't know a genuine feeling if it bit them."

Hades sculled the rest of his cognac and slammed the glass on the table. "It was the way things were, and nothing now will ever change that. You were a horndog who proved to be a shit of a father, although not as bad as ours admittedly. Now you have a loving mate and two adorable children. The Fates gave you a second chance."

"They gave you one too." This time when Sei reached over, his hand rested over Hades' wrist. Hades stared at Sei's elegant fingers. He couldn't remember the last time one of his family members willingly touched him. "Ali is perfect for you brother, and I'm sure you and he will spend eternity in blissful happiness. But if you need a friend, a true brother...."

"Then I know where you are." Hades nodded. He paused a moment, then said. "My Ali tells me that when people hang out, they are supposed to talk about interests they have in common. As I'm not about to share what Ali and I get up to in the bedroom, why don't you tell me more about what your older sons, and your two newest children have been up to?"

A cute line ran across Sei's forehead. "You and Ali don't have children and aren't likely to have any. How can my children be a shared interest?"

"Maybe because we're related? They are my nephews and niece."

"Oh yeah." Sei's smile had a goofy tinge to it. "Well, let's see. You know Artemas and Silvanus are together. Well, they…."

Hades poured himself another drink and leaned back in his chair. Sei's recounting of his children's lives washed over him, setting off feelings he'd never felt around his brother before. By the time Ali and Claude joined them, the cognac bottle was empty, but Hades had worked out what that feeling was. It was acceptance and for Hades, it was a heady feeling and one he hoped he would enjoy for a long time to come.

Chapter Twenty Four

Two weeks later and Ali should have been happy. Thanks to a few well-placed calls by Claude, and some sniffing around from the Tulsa enforcers, all the young people enslaved by Arthur and Thorn were found, and were now safe. Arthur took Hades' words to heart, and turned himself into the shifter council and the last Ali had heard from Larry, he was in culinary school.

Miranda sold the house, lands, and businesses and had disappeared. The family based scurry was disbanded after numerous members of Ali's extended family had been found guilty of a huge list of crimes. Ali could sleep easily, knowing no one he was related to was going to hurt anyone again.

Life with Hades couldn't be more perfect. Ali's loving mate had accepted his suggestions for making changes to the way hardened souls were sentenced. Given how the level of crimes had increased over the years, Folsom's flowchart had been expanded. Mass murderers and other crimes that had been rare fifty years ago, were now treated as more commonplace, and new automatic sentences had been added.

The Furies still handled anyone who committed crimes involving children, but now Hades didn't have to sit in on that judgment. A simple tick in a set of boxes on the new form Ali devised had everything streamlined, so Hades only had to have a court date once a month for "unusual" cases.

Baby still hadn't been heard from again, but Hades said that wasn't unusual. The two men visited Hades' nephews and their mates – Lasse, Artemas, and even Nereus who lived in the Cloverleah pack. Ali had enjoyed a fun-filled afternoon there, bouncing on the heads and nipping the tails of the shifters who were happy to play with him in his fur. With wolves, bears, a giant cat, and even a dragon, Ali's chipmunk's world had suddenly evolved into a huge furry obstacle course, but with Hades watching over them, Ali never felt safer. Back in the Underworld, Juno, the hellhound thought it was a great honor to have Ali's chipmunk form ride on his head as they paraded around the gates some days.

So, life was perfect. Letting out a huff, Ali plucked at the feather coverlets Hades ordered especially for their bedroom. The big man himself had disappeared from their bed earlier that morning, off to quell some demon riot, which was probably no more than a squabble between two families. Ali found most of the demons easy to deal with. They loved to fight among themselves, but when Ali had instigated a new incentive scheme for them, allowing any demon to earn the right to make more visits to the earth realm, the number of fights had dropped dramatically. No one wanted to give up their chance to shop, or at least, that was Folsom's plan. One of the mansion guards Ali befriended, Braxas, said he enjoyed visiting the earth realm so he could sit in a park and enjoy the quiet and the sunshine. Surprised at his candor, Ali agreed that was a perfect way to spend the afternoon.

He wasn't bored. Nope. The twinge in Ali's ass let him know he'd been used hard and he'd loved every minute of it. A lazy morning was exactly what he needed. But... but... there it was again. That damn howling. Ali had been listening to it all morning and it was setting his teeth on edge.

"Damn dog," he muttered as he scrabbled out of bed. In the bathroom he did nothing more than necessary, except for a quick splash of water on his face. Yes, he stunk of sex and Hades but if he was going to confront Cerberus his scent would say far more than words ever could.

Nodding at Braxas who was stationed outside their room, Ali hurried towards the main entrance. Heavy boots let him know he wasn't alone. Looking over his shoulder at Braxas he smiled. "I'm fine, just going to speak to Cerberus. You don't have to come."

"My Lord's exact words were 'if the Consort leaves our private quarters, make sure you don't let him out of your sight'. Sorry, boss. I can't ignore a direct order."

"He does worry about me." Ali said fondly. He wasn't about to get Braxas into trouble with Hades. "Come on, then, although I don't plan on getting close enough to that dog for him to bite me."

"Cerberus had been spoiled," Braxas confided. "Before he fucked up, he and Hades shared a mind link and everything. The damn dog used to boast about it."

Ouch. Ali was determined Braxas wouldn't know how badly the comment about the mind link hurt him. Although he could pick up snippets of what his mate was thinking on occasion, like when he'd passed out at his father's house, the ability to converse with each other in secret had so far eluded them.

"Hades mentioned Cerberus kidnapped Lasse and tried to kill him?"

"I'm not sure the silly dog would have actually killed him, but Lasse was trussed up hanging over the firepit in the throne room at one point." Braxas leaned over Ali's shoulder opening the door for him; a surprisingly gentlemanly move from someone who stood over seven foot tall, had black scales and a tail that had to be five foot long.

"Does anyone know why Cerberus did it? I mean, if he was loyal enough to escape the pits where his brother ended up, and you say Hades spoiled him, then... why?"

Braxas, to his credit didn't just blurt out a bunch of gossip like Folsom would have done. He seemed to be genuinely trying to answer the question. "You're a shifter, right?"

"I seem to recall you caught me sitting in my fur eating cherries off the dining room table just last week." Ali grinned.

Braxas's laugh bounced through the air. "True enough, sir. But do you ever, you know, have a problem where your human side doesn't agree with your chipmunk's ideas?"

"I can't say that's ever happened, no." Ali frowned. "Are you telling me Cerberus is a shifter? Does his human half have three heads too?"

"No, sir," Braxas chuckled at the idea. "His human half has one very thick head. In demon terms I'm not that old, but word has it, Cerberus was born a dog, or created or however he came into being. He must have been born, because Lord Hades has had him since he was a pup. I did hear, and this is secondhand mind you, that things weren't going well with Lady Persephone at the time, and Lord Hades allowed Cerberus to have a human form to reward his loyalty. That was eons before I was born though."

"I bet you were a cute baby," Ali grinned. "So, is that what you think happened to Cerberus – his two sides are at war with each other?"

Wandering around the side of the mansion to where Cerberus was being held, Braxas winced as the dog howled again. "I'm sure no one knows what goes on in that dog's mind. But his human half longed for Lord Hades to recognize him as a mate, while his puppy half is still as devoted and loyal as ever. I reckon that's why he howls. He misses his master."

"That is so sad." Now Ali understood why Cerberus's chains bothered him so much. Being confined for any shifter was a form of hell in itself. "Cerberus," he called out strongly. "That's enough howling. I want to talk to you."

Three heads snapped in his direction. Jowls drooling, bright red eyes flashing and nostrils flaring. "My Lord has soiled himself with you." The snarl was guttural and rough.

"If you mean my Lord and mate made love to me all night, then yes, you're right." Ali refused to feel intimidated. "That is part of being mates as I am sure you're aware."

"Mates." The middle head snarled while growls rumbled from the other two. "My Lord must have been lonely indeed to take up with you. You're not worthy of a god."

"Normally, I'd agree with you, but not this time." Ali motioned for Braxas to fetch him a chair. He'd learned to click up a cushion all by himself. "Hades has been alone for more time than I can comprehend. Doesn't it mean anything to you that I make him happy?"

It was weird watching three sets of eyes glancing at each other. "I made him happy until you came along," the middle head said at last.

Ali tilted his head to one side and eyed the huge beast. "Bullshit. You were in chains when we met. And yet, I remember how stories told of how the great Cerberus guarded the gates and was loyal only to his master. Now, the gates are watched by hellhounds. That doesn't sound like the loyal Cerberus I heard of."

"I have always been loyal to my lord. None have been with him longer than I have."

Ali tapped the side of his nose. "I'm a shifter remember. I can scent your lies." Crossing one leg over the other, and refusing to think how silly he might look, sitting on a chair just out of snapping distance from a story-book sized beast who could easily take his head off. "I wasn't aware you were a shifter. Those chains must be difficult for you."

"My master will let me out eventually. He has a good heart."

"That's true." Ali nodded. "However, I know Hades is thinking of sending you to Tartarus, just like your brother. Trying to kill me wasn't your best move, if you want to be free."

"He should be happy with me." The three heads swung around, snarling and snapping at nothing.

"He was happy with you, as his faithful hound," Ali yelled, not sure if Cerberus would listen, but the snarling stopped instantly.

"He was?" Three long necks twined around each other as if they sought comfort from each other.

"Of course, he was. Everyone the world over knows of the loyal Cerberus who would lay down his life for his Master and who protects the Underworld."

"People actually know about me?"

"Yes, they do. I learned who you were when I was at school. I bet if anyone could see you now, they'd be so disappointed."

There was a long silence. "My brother said my Master didn't want me anymore. My Lord was away from the realm so often and he'd blocked his link with me."

That damn mind link, although Ali was starting to get an inkling why theirs didn't work as well as it should. "Hades was looking for me," he said gently. "You have such an important job, and Hades cares for you as his hound but he needed to be mated with someone who could be happy with him anywhere. Don't you see, the only reason Hades could stay away so often, was because he trusted you and his demons to run things while he was away."

A whimpering dog is always a pitiful sound, but whimpers from three mouths was heartbreaking. "I should never have listened to my brother." Cerberus was crying now – gulping, heaving coughs and snarls, snot drooling from his nostrils and slobber falling from his three jaws.

Ali looked away. He wasn't sure he could conjure a handkerchief big enough to clean all that snot. Besides, he felt sorry for the overgrown puppy. As he sat and waited for the storm to pass, he felt the growing presence of his mate. If he was going to act, he was going to have to do it quickly.

"Cerberus," he said urgently. "Can you say, paw on heart, that you're truly sorry for what you did to Lasse, and for how you deceived your Master that one time?"

"It was only once." Cerberus hiccupped.

"Exactly, it was only once, and no one got badly hurt. You've had centuries of loyal service that should be taken into account. I am sure Hades would have forgiven you by now, but you tried to kill me, and he won't ever let you go if he thinks you're a danger to me or to his rule."

"I wouldn't be," Cerberus said with a hitch in his voice. "I miss my life. I want to be my Master's loyal hound again. I was safe that way."

Ali inhaled sharply. Hades was near. This was it. "You know if Hades didn't punish you then he'd look weak and that would damage his reputation."

"I don't want that," Cerberus said showing puppy dog eyes which was more disconcerting than it sounded seeing as there were six of them.

"You are happy as a hound."

All three heads bobbed up and down.

Ali leaned forward, resting his elbows on his knees. "What if, as your punishment, Hades removed your ability to shift into a human form? You could still be the faithful hound, but you would never walk on two legs again."

Or have the ability to seduce my mate. But Ali dismissed that thought as soon as he had it. Cerberus had never learned to be human, hadn't grown up with the advantages Ali had. But it was the human side of Cerberus that was the problem – which was why Cerberus howled all the time. Locked in his puppy form, Cerberus's animal instincts just missed being with his Master.

"Could I... would I still be able to talk to him if you took my human body away?"

How the hell should I know? But Ali trusted his mate, so he nodded. "You'd still have to communicate with the demon guards. Hades would still want to talk to you when we're doing our rounds. You just wouldn't have your human side to shift into which means you'd never be able to leave the realm again."

Ali could see the indecision. The quiver of Cerberus's giant shoulders gave him away. "But my master leaves so often."

"He would be with me and our friends. Nothing will happen to him."

"You would protect him?"

Ignoring the note of incredulity Ali nodded. "I'm immortal, just like he is. Nothing can kill me."

"I tried to."

"And if you want to be set free it would be best if you didn't try that again," Ali said firmly. "Just think of it. No human concerns, no strange feelings you don't know how to cope with. Just being able to enjoy your life as the famous hound of the Underworld, showing loyalty to Hades and our realm through your devoted service and your fierce nature."

"I miss you like that, Cerberus," Hades said, suddenly appearing behind Ali's chair. "I miss seeing my beloved hound guarding the gates as he has done for all time."

"Master, oh Master, please." Cerberus's whole body wriggled, and his necks stretched as he tried to breach the distance between them.

"No more shifting. I think my mate has a very good idea, don't you?"

"I'll take the punishment, my Lord and Master, please just let me out of these chains."

Ali felt the weight of Hades' hand on his shoulder only briefly as his mate stepped past, walking right up to Cerberus's bulk. "I can't have a hound who won't be loyal to me and my mate."

"I swear my loyalty to you and the Consort Ali. Should I err in my oath, I'll throw myself in the eternal fires myself. You have my word."

"If you break your oath, I'll throw you in myself. This is the last chance you get." Reaching up, Hades stretched his arms encompassing all three heads. The muttered words were too low for Ali to hear but Cerberus yelped, just once, before he sagged against his chains.

"It is done," Hades said. "I think giving you a dual form was my mistake from the start." He reached up brushing his hands against the huge collar attached to the chains, causing it to break and fall to the ground. "You have always been a precious hound. Don't let me down."

"Master, oh thank you Master," Cerberus growled and yipped as he pranced around, circling, running, circling back to Hades again. "Command me, Master," he begged, nudging close for a pat that Hades seemed happy to give.

"Your place is at the gates, my hound. Let none pass who should not enter."

"Thank yooooooooou." The howl drifted through the breeze as Cerberus sprinted for the gates, his heads already moving from side to side as though he was already on guard.

Chapter Twenty Five

"Did Sei tell you why he wanted to see us specifically tonight?"

Hades looked up from buckling his boots to see Ali coming out of the bathroom. Wearing nothing but a towel wrapped around his slender hips. Hades bit the inside of his lip. Nothing made his cock perk up faster than his half-clad mate. Doing his best to focus on the question, an effort made harder when Ali just dropped his towel and sauntered naked over to the dressing table. The dressing table that within touching distance. "He, er, Sei asked if he could borrow a few of my closest demons. I don't know why. But we're meeting him in his realm which will be something different for you."

"Have you ever been there?" Ali's ass wiggled as he pulled on a pair of well fitting pants. "How weird would it be, living under the sea all the time. What if the roof of his house caved in?"

"Then Sei would morph into his god of the sea form, which is about four times bigger than how he appears at Claude's club, and swim to safety." Straightening up, Hades nudged his dick into a more comfortable position. "Babe, Sei's realm is like this one. It's not like you can point to a place on a map like you can with Artemas's house in Australia, and say that's where Poseidon lives. As the Underworld is a realm apart, but tied to earth, Sei's realm is part of the sea, but isn't, if that makes sense."

"Not at all," Ali said cheerfully buttoning up his shirt. "Those are the ways of gods, that mortals like me aren't meant to understand. Although," he added, as his hands dropped and his voice deepened, "there are some things I understand about you very well. Shall I bother with the buttons on this shirt, or are you going to ravage me?"

Hades groaned. "I would love to ravage you, my sweetness, but as Gods rarely get the right to go into another's domain, we need to leave in the next five minutes, or we won't get in. And it would take a lot longer than five minutes to do all I want to do to you."

"Finish getting me dressed then." Ali stepped into his space. Hades' arms slid around him as if he had no choice, his hands automatically smoothing down his mate's sleek back and settling on the perky orbs of his butt. *You're going to leave me with a mess in my pants,* Hades leaned into the kiss Ali was expecting. That was another thing that had improved about their mating. Ali explained, after arranging for Hades to set Cerberus free, that the reason their mind link was so spasmodic, was a part of Hades was blocking him, when he meant to be blocking Cerberus. Fixing the issue was as simple as Hades accepting Ali in his mind because he had every right to be there.

And now, as Ali flung his arms around his neck, his body stretched out with his toes barely on the ground, Hades was grateful. It meant he could kiss and suck to his heart's content and still let Ali know, with words, just how much he was loved and cherished. Which he did until the annoying beep on his watch reminded them both they had places to be.

"We'll finish this later, my love." Hades pulled back, loving the passion Ali showed so openly.

"Either that, or we'll get Sei to point us in the direction of the bathroom, and finish this in there."

"Let's feed you first." Hades didn't let on how much he was keen on that idea. Holding his mate close, Hades focused on his brother, trusting their link to have him relocate in the right place. As they appeared in Sei's realm, Hades looked around and his mouth dropped open. It wasn't the stone walls, or the large portholes showing the sea life going on outside of them that shocked him. It was all the people who were sitting around a huge table that was laden down with food from around the world.

"What is this?" Hades hung onto his mate tightly. Poseidon and Claude, he expected. But there were so many other faces he recognized – Thanatos and his mate. Thor and Orin were there. Sebastian, his nephews and their mates. Folsom and Braxas representing the Underworld, Folsom looking natty in his purple shirt that actually complemented his green skin. Even Ra, Helios and Abraxas were chatting around the big table. All looked up at him expectantly, all with huge smiles on their faces.

"I don't get it. What is this?"

"This, my dear brother, is your mating celebration," Sei said. He strode over and before Hades knew what was happening his brother was hugging him. As soon as Sei was finished with him, Claude was there doing the same thing!

"I did listen to you that day," Sei said, "and yeah, it might have taken a bit of time, but I reached out to all the people who knew you best, and... this is it. Your party, full of people who care about you, and who know how much good you do for all of us and our realms, by keeping us safe. Consider this your extended family if you will."

The only reason Hades was still upright was because Ali was plastered to his side. Scanning the faces once more. "So many missing," he whispered, noticing that Zeus, and his other siblings hadn't bothered to show up.

"It's the people who came here that count, my friend," Claude said with a smile. "Focus on the positive."

Hades blinked once, twice, and then a third time. Then standing proud and tall, he said in a voice that reached all corners of the room. "My friends, thank you all so much for being here. For those of you who haven't met him yet, this wonderful man beside me is Ali, Lord of the Underworld and my most precious gift from the Fates. He is, without doubt, the light in my soul, and I can't thank you enough for being here to celebrate his arrival in our family. Now let's eat. We don't want my brother's efforts to go to waste."

Laughter and a few claps sounded as Sei and Claude led them to their chairs. Hades stopped for a moment between Ra and Helios. "I'm grateful you both came here, but is it wise to have two sun gods sitting so close together?" Ali's chuckle helped lighten his words.

"Lord Hades." Ra inclined his head gracefully. "Though our sun might not reach your domain, that does not mean we don't think of you often. When Helios mentioned he and Abraxas were coming, I felt someone had to represent my pantheon and who better than me. While others might only think of you as the badass of the Underworld, I saw you often enough on earth to know you were a good man, saddled with a difficult task."

"My load is a lot easier now." Hades managed a smile. "Ali's smiles rival the sun itself, and in the Underworld he has charmed all he sees, including Cerberus."

"Who are you? If you don't mind me asking that is," Ali said, proving Hades' statement with a smile of his own.

Getting up from his chair, Ra wasn't much taller than Ali. He bowed low. "I am Ra, Egyptian god of the sun. My companion is Helios, the Greek god of the sun who rides his chariot daily bringing light to the masses."

"And one of Helios's horses is Abraxas," Ali waved at the handsome man who was sitting further around the table. "I remember now. Wow, you have no idea how exciting this is for me. Gods I've only read about at our mating celebration."

"There's a few here," Ra laughed as he moved so he was standing on the other side of Ali. "Let's see. I'm sure you know Artemas and Silvanus, both gods in their own right, although Silvanus is the oldest guy at the table today."

"Old enough to smack your butt if you keep being cheeky," Silvanus smiled and waved, Artemas looking at him adoringly next to him.

"Sei, of course is the god of the sea, while you know his mate is the son of Fenrir, and then we have Thor, Norse god of the storms." Ra pointed them out.

"That guy is Thor? He's massive," Ali whispered.

"It's not him you have to watch," Hades said quietly. "His mate, Orin, holds the only spell capable of summoning a god. Really friendly guy, although very protective of their children as a parent should be."

"They've managed to have children too? Oh, Hades." Ali looked up, his teeth caught in his bottom lip. "I'm so sorry that won't happen for us."

"Actually, that might not be true." Silvanus got to his feet. "If you'd all like to take your seats, everyone. I have a message from the Mother."

Who's the Mother? Ali asked through their link. *Is that Silvanus's mother or....*

The mother of all life. The reason life exists. Moving over to the only two empty spaces Hades held Ali's chair for him and then slid into the one next to it.

"My friends, we are here on a truly wonderful occasion, to celebrate the mating of Hades and Ali." Silvanus smiled as he looked around the table. "The Fates have finally heard our call. Too long have gods fretted alone, living lives without purpose now the need for us has waned. But I look at so many of you now with loving mates of your own." He winked at Ra and Helios. "One can be assured the Fates work is not over yet."

Good natured chuckles rang around the room and Helios and Ra were subject to a few nudges.

"It is perhaps also significant," Silvanus continued when the noise died down, "that at this table are both the representatives of life through me and my mate, and death." He inclined his head to Thanatos who nodded. "Out of all of us, Hades and Thanatos have had the most difficult tasks, for one can only imagine how any mortal clings so fiercely to the life granted by the Mother."

"Some are more difficult than others," Cody, Thanatos's mate called out hotly. "You should see the mess my mate comes home in sometimes." Hades had only met the sweet shifter once, but he knew how fiercely protective Cody was of his mate. Knowing his back story, Hades was pleased to see how much the young man had gained his confidence.

Silvanus smiled and opened his hands to indicate everyone. "We, all of us, appreciate that fortunes change on the human world. Many of us have been frustrated by the non-intervention law, yet to prevent widespread destruction we've bit our tongues and buried our feelings. For most people the only certainty with life anymore, is eventual death, with the exception of those at this table."

More laughter and Hades took the time to look around the gathering. Sure enough, everyone, either by birth or through mating, had been granted immortality. The warm glow he felt inside was nothing to do with Ali's hand on his thigh, but more from a feeling that he knew now the rest of his eternal life would be filled with friends and family members. He glanced down at Ali who was beaming at him.

Silvanus wasn't finished. "When Artemas and I claimed each other, the Mother, in her infinite wisdom blessed my mate with carrying the Tree of Life. For the first time in centuries, that tree is growing, bringing with it, new hope for the future. It is with that in mind, that I bring the Mother's blessings to this table. Ali, Cody, Raff, Teilo and Madison, can you all stand please?"

Ali's hand tightened on Hades' thigh. "It's okay, my love," Hades whispered softly. "None will harm you here."

"But he's got a message from *the* Mother," Ali whispered back frantically. "You've met my mother. There was nothing good about her."

"This one's different." Hades urged his mate to stand. Looking around the table he wasn't the only one concerned about his mate.

"This may come as a shock," Silvanus said with a wry smile. "As we all know, procreation has, until now, been restricted between male/female couples. Admittedly, the gods got around that. Two people, with a direct claim to a god line could conceive, regardless of gender. But for paranormals and humans alike, the gender restrictions applied. For the most part they still do – more a question of biology and science, than anything to do with the concepts of life itself."

"Get on with it, Silva," Artemas said with a grin and a nudge to his mate. "I swear, you take any opportunity you can to lecture people about the meaning of life. These guys are standing here terrified and the food is getting cold."

A warm pink blush spread over Silvanus's cheeks. "My apologies. Put simply, the blessing from the Mother, should you choose to accept it, is that you men will be granted the same rights to procreation as if you had been born into the god-line yourself.

What that means, is regardless of how you conduct yourself in the bedroom...."

"He means it doesn't matter if you top or bottom," Sei called out.

"You will be able to either father a child with your mate, or have the ability to get pregnant yourselves." Silvanus held out his hands. "The choice will always be yours; the Mother doesn't seek to change that. But as the human populations swell, to keep things balanced, she believes it is only fair that any person joined with a god, regardless of gender or genetics, should be able to share in a loving family around them, and the Fates agreed."

"Oh, my freaking god. I can get pregnant?" Ali slumped in his chair. A burst of chatter sprung up around them, but Hades only had eyes for his mate.

"You wanted children," he reminded Ali quietly, pulling his mate onto his lap and cuddling him close.

"I sorta did, but I didn't, because of my family, and then…. Oh shit. We already said it didn't matter that we couldn't."

"And if you don't want them, then we don't have to have them," Hades tilted his mate's face up so he could watch his face. "Silvanus said the choice was ours. The Fates recognize intent. We can go on as we have so far, and I'll be just as happy as I am now. But if you did, you know, ever think you might want children with me, then I wouldn't have a problem with carrying them for us."

Ali's eyes widened so far, his eyebrows almost disappeared in his hair line. His mouth was a perfect 'O'. Hades wanted to laugh, but the moment was too serious.

"You'd let us switch things around." Ali glanced around, as if making sure no one was listening. But with the momentous news Silvanus had given them all, no one was paying attention to them. Ali leaned closer. "You'd let me do you?"

Hades nodded.

"And by do, you know I mean dooooo you."

Hades nodded again.

Ali leaned back and fanned his face with his hand. "You know, I've coped with some freaky shit since I've met you. The Underworld, Persephone, demons, Cerberus, the Pits, the Furies who still freak me out, learning my family were not only assholes but criminals of the worst kind and now this. Children."

Hades swallowed the nudge of worry that lodged in his gut. "If this is all too much for you, Silvanus said the Mother always intended the choice to be ours. We don't have to if you don't want to."

"Are you nuts, and I don't mean the kind I normally nibble?" Stretching up, Ali whispered in Hades' ear. "All I want to know is how long will it take to get us out of this party. I want you back in our room in the Underworld, where we won't be interrupted. I want your gorgeous naked body spread out over the edge of the bed with that pale butt of yours sticking in the air so I can lick it and nibble it, driving you wild until you beg me to sink my dick into your tightest and most intimate place."

Hades swallowed hard. His asshole twitched as if he could already imagine how it would feel, to be possessed that way. "An hour longer should do it," he said, noting his voice was raspy. "Eat quickly and we should be out of here in an hour."

Chapter Twenty Six

It was actually closer to four hours before Hades whisked them back to the Underworld. After the first half hour, where Ali was so horny, he thought his cock would burst if he moved the wrong way, he found he really didn't mind. For someone used to being on his own, Hades seemed to open up the longer they sat there, and for Ali, talking to the gods he'd learned about at school was amazing.

Thor was a surprise, pulling out a long line of photos of his twin boys and sharing stories involving dirty diapers and spew on his shoulder. Orin, his mate, was just as friendly. Ali found himself making plans with them to have dinner the following week, in Manhattan. *Another place I haven't been.* Abraxas was jolly, hugging on his tiny mate Jordan anytime he could. What surprised Ali was how Jordan had no problems teasing Sei, even though it must have been really uncomfortable for him, knowing that two of the other party members were the result of Sei and Abraxas's affair.

But with good wishes speeding their trip home, Hades and Ali were finally alone. Their bedroom was silent in comparison to the party scene. Hades lit the fire, and turned on one of the bedside lamps. Nervousness was pulsing through their bond. "Did you... do you think we should shower first?" Hades asked and Ali was struck by how tentative he sounded.

The reason why hit him with a blinding flash. Running over, Ali jumped. Hades always caught him. Stroking down the side of the face Ali loved more than life itself, he shook his head. "Why didn't you tell me you hadn't done this before, babe?"

Hades gave that half shrug he used when he was embarrassed but didn't want to say so. "I'm the big badass Lord of the Underworld. It's not as though anyone was going to come up to me and say, 'bend over' now, is it?"

"Oh, babe, I would've done if I thought you'd say yes." Ali peppered kisses along his mate's rigid jaw. "We'll take it slow. You can use your magic if it makes you more comfortable. Anything you want, anything at all. I just want it to be good for you."

"It already is." Ali was conscious of the heat of Hades' hands on his ass. "I trust you."

"Aw, now you're making me feel all mushy," Ali teased. Unhooking his legs from Hades' hips, he slid down his mate's body. Reaching up, he slowly started unbuttoning Hades' shirt, the heat in his body rising as more and more pale skin was revealed.

Hades stood like a statue, the only sign he was affected bulging the front of his black pants. With the shirt buttons undone, Ali stretched, easing the shirt off Hades' shoulders and letting it fall to the floor. Then sinking down on first one knee and then two, Ali pressed his face into the front of Hades' pants, nuzzling the bulge he could feel underneath.

"You smell so good all the time," he murmured, his hands reaching down to unbuckle Hades' boots. "But here... hmmm..." He let the material of the pants brush against his cheeks, first one side and then the other. "Intoxicating. Step out." He tapped on Hades' boots.

With his boots off, and his chest heaving ever so slightly, Ali was sure he'd never seen anyone so magnificent. He stayed, on his knees, breathing in the scent of Hades' crotch, his nose nudging at the mounds where his mate's balls were confined by the material, mouthing along the thick length that stretched down Hades' left leg.

"Wouldn't this be better with my pants off?" Hades moaned, and from the corner of his eye, Ali noticed his fists were clenched.

"Hmm, could be." Ali deftly undid the button on the top of Hades' pants, before sliding the zipper down inch by inch. "I just love your skin here." He pushed his face in the opening of Hades' pants, licking the freshly bared skin, leaving the zipper nestling just above the jut of his mate's cock.

"Ali!"

Ali could take a hint. Being careful, because zippers could have sharp edges, he gently eased the rest of the zip down and tugged the pants open all the way. Reaching inside, he tugged at Hades' length, easing it free, pushing the pants underneath Hades' balls. Hades' sigh of relief was evident.

Studying Hades' cock, Ali relearned it all over again. The thick long shaft curving slightly to the left. Silky smooth skin covering it, right up to where the foreskin was already unable to contain the almost purple head. Pale clear droplets formed at the slit and Ali captured them with his tongue, groaning as Hades' unique flavor coated his taste buds. Lapping them up, he used his hand to pump out more, dipping the tip of his tongue in the slit so not a drop was wasted.

"Bed. Ali. Please. My knees won't hold me."

Giving Hades' cock one last kiss, Ali jumped up, pulling off his clothes not caring where they fell. In the meantime, Hades shucked off his pants and climbed onto the bed.

"How do you want me?"

"Oh, Babe, I'm not as callous as that." Ali climbed up after him, moving up so he could cradle Hades' head in his hands. "I love you so much, my mate."

Hades might have said something similar, but Ali didn't give him a chance. Leaning over, Ali poured all the emotion he could into their kiss. His love, his passion for his mate, even the niggling worry he had about them being parents. Hades moaned and his body writhed under the onslaught.

Ten minutes passed. Fifteen. Who cared? Ali definitely didn't. He loved the feeling of Hades' skin against his, the way his body moved under his hands, and how his lips scorched something deep inside of him. His cock, which had been hard for what felt like days, hardened further thanks to all the stimulation, but Ali didn't want to stop. In all the chaos in his new life, Hades was the one constant and Ali wanted to keep kissing his mate until his lips bled.

Hades had a different idea. "Sweetness," he gasped, dragging their lips apart. "I'm ready. You have to. Now. Please."

Ali rolled flat on his back, holding out his cock from his body. "This will be easier," he urged. "Take it at your own pace. Slowly. No sudden moves… oomph."

So, this is what it's like having a god sit on my dick. Ali froze. Hades hadn't waited. Ali barely had time to move his hand away. And now his mate must be really uncomfortable because the searing heat and tightness around Ali's cock was excruciating. Holding Hades' hips firm, Ali counted in his head, breathing slowly in and out, wondering if his cock was still connected to his body.

Pain didn't show on Hades' face – his mate wasn't like that. But the badass of the Underworld looked as though he didn't dare twitch. His beautifully hard cock had wilted under the strain, and keeping his movements slow, Ali slid his hands over Hades' thigh and gently stroked the flaccid organ to life again.

"There you go," he crooned as Hades' breathing became more regular and the cock in his hand firmed up. "Someone needs to read an anal sex manual, and learn that one can't just jump on their mate's cock as if they're jumping into a saddle. Something like that tends to hurt."

"Just a smidgeon," Hades panted. "Give me a minute."

It wasn't as though Ali could move if he wanted to. The grip around his shaft meant he wasn't going anywhere. Instead, he focused on raising Hades' arousal again. It didn't take long, but Ali finally felt the tightness around his length ease.

"Oh yes," Hades said rocking slightly. "That's... that's a lot better now."

"You're in control," Ali whispered, as he tried to push up with his hips.

"Nice and steady, move the way you want to."

"Oh, I want." Hades' looked down. Ali was pleased to see the lust shining bright in his eyes again. Keeping his grasp of Hades' cock nice and even, the two men moved together, slowly at first, but as the precome started leaking from his cock again, Hades' movements got faster. He wriggled slightly, one side to the other. "There it is, oh wow, I've never felt anything like it."

If it'd been anyone but his mate, Ali might have taken objection to the way his body was being used as a sex toy – one of those that had a sucky bottom that could stick to stuff while the user backs up to it and fucks himself on it. But it was Hades, who was magnificent in every way just by virtue of his existence.

In his passion, however, Hades became so much more – relaxed, yet in control. Open. Free of the masks he saw fit to wear on any given day. Ali loved every aspect of his mate, but seeing him like this, the veins in his neck taut as he threw his head back, sweat gleaming off his chest, as his thigh muscles worked to keep his ass moving.

Ali's breath quickened. The cock moving through his hands got harder, and still he couldn't take his eyes off his mate. His chipmunk came through, seeing through his eyes, watching as their mate took his pleasure. It was a proud moment, a special event. Ali waited, he waited, and then it came, or rather Hades did. The smell of warm spunk hit Ali's nose, as his chest was coated in the stuff. Hades' ass muscles clamped tight, and Ali yelled as his cock unloaded deep into his mate.

"Oh fuck. Oh fuck." Hades dropped his hands down, so they were resting on the mattress on either side of Ali's head. "Don't move, please don't make me move for a minute."

"Are you okay?" Ali was still panting. It wasn't as though he wanted to go anywhere.

A smile, softer than Ali had ever seen before, graced his mate's beautiful face. "I'm trying to make a baby stick."

Oh wow. Yep. Now Ali definitely couldn't move. He doubted his legs would hold him up if he tried.

/~/~/~/~/

It was a few hours later. Both men had been cleaned, eaten a light supper and then crawled back into bed. Ali was where Hades liked him to be, curled up in his arms, snuffling softly as he slept. As for Hades, he wasn't sure if sleep was even possible, the events of the evening replaying themselves over and over in his head.

We could have our own baby. Even now, Ali's hand was resting on his stomach as if trying to encourage tiny cells to grow. Hades had worried about Silvanus's announcement, not for himself, but for how Ali might feel. Hades had grown up knowing that babies between male couples was possible in the god line. He'd just never found a male god he was remotely attracted to.

When he dragged Persephone into his life, the desire for children sunk even further. Hades hated the way she behaved when she was in the Underworld, and couldn't imagine having kids with her, even if she had let him touch her. And then Ali came along, without a glimmer of god genetics in his blood and Hades squashed any hopes he had for children and gave thanks for the gift he had received.

I have hope, he realized as he patted the hand Ali had rested on him. *I have love, friends, a connection with one of my brothers, and I have hope. Hope for a brighter future.*

"You're thinking too much," Ali said sleepily. "If you're growing a baby, you need your rest. Love you." He snuggled further under the blankets and started to snore again.

Hades smiled, settling down just as Ali asked him to. The chances of getting pregnant the first time was remote, but now Hades knew it could happen. One weird thought crossed his mind as he drifted off – *I wonder how many of the others blessed by the Mother tonight were doing what we did? Imagine a whole group of godly babies all growing up at the same time.* Hades thought that was a nice idea, but then he was asleep and dreamed of soft cuddly babies and drool on his shoulder.

Epilogue

Four months later

The sun was soft on Hades' skin as he watched his mate's tiny chipmunk form scamper over a fallen log and come running up to him, climbing on his belly and up to his chest, chittering madly.

"I never did learn Chipmunk," Hades said with a smile that appeared more often now. "If I had to guess what you were saying, I think you're probably telling me off for eating the last of the crackers. There's fruit in the picnic basket, you don't have to go nutty at me. Here, let me get it."

The rapid chittering and a thump of a furry foot on Hades' chest stopped him moving. "I'm pregnant, not an invalid," he said as he sank back down into the long grass. They were in Greece, enjoying the last of the summer before Hades started to show too much and would have to restrict who he could see. Or more to the point, who might see him.

"We can't stay too much longer," Hades said as he watched Ali's furry butt disappear into the picnic hamper. "Thanatos and Cody are coming for dinner and I think Sebastian and Madison are too. Did you ever imagine it – Sebastian being the pregnant one in that relationship? Although, from what Thanatos was saying, Madison's planning a huge baby sex reveal party next week and he won't let Sebastian do anything to help."

Ali's cute face shot up, peering over the edge of the basket, his cheeks working furiously.

"You found the fruit I got for you then. Ah." Stretching one arm over his head, Hades sprawled out. "This is wonderful. Helios is working overtime today."

"More like Abraxas is running hard to get home to his mate." Ali's naked body slid up the grass beside him. "There won't be many days like this left. Another week or two and summer will be behind us."

"We can visit Artemas and Silvanus in Australia," Hades sighed in contentment. "It'll still be warm down there."

"You have an added bonus with fall this year," Ali said resting his head on Hades' belly. "The dying leaves won't signify the beginning of three months with Persephone in the Underworld."

"That's true too. Just you and me and Folsom insisting he needs another trip to the earth realm to buy items for the nursery."

"We'll have to start hiring him out," Ali said sleepily. "He can become a godly nursery personal shopper or something."

"Don't you go to sleep," Hades flicked him lightly on the shoulder. "I told you, we've got company for dinner tonight."

"Got room for one more at the dinner table, Uncle?"

Hades shot up, clicking his fingers so Ali was dressed. On the other side of the picnic basket was Baby, and it looked as though he might have been crying.

"Baby, what the hell? Are you hurt? What's wrong?"

"I need a pregnancy test," Baby burst into tears, sinking to his knees. "I think my mate got me pregnant."

The End, or more fairly, To Be Continued.

****

Thank you so much to all my lovely readers for reaching the end of this story. I do hope you enjoyed it. And YES! The next book in this series will be Baby's story, although the timeline with that book and this one will overlap slightly. I'm not a meanie and I wouldn't start a book with Baby mated and pregnant without letting you know how it happened. So, Baby's book will start roughly around the time he left the Underworld after getting upset at dinner and go from there.

I really enjoyed writing Hades' and Ali's book. It might not have been filled with as much angst as some of my readers might have been expecting – after all, a lot of this book was set in the Underworld. But that might have been because of Ali – he was just so sweet and yet he had such a strong spirit, and I just knew he'd be perfect for bringing Hades out of his shell.

If you enjoyed this story, would you please consider leaving a review. Thanks to changes in social media algorithms, promoting stories is getting more and more difficult, particularly for MM authors. A short review can make all the difference for new readers coming across my stories.

I believe it was Ali in this story who mentioned there is a lot of hate spreading around the world at the moment. I see evidence of it every day in the news, and it's not always easy to shut it out. But good people, like you and me, we can do our best to combat it in tiny ways every single day. Share your smile with a stranger as you walk down the street, pay that cup of coffee forward, give your partner random flowers for no other reason than because you care. Forget the washing up and spend half an hour playing with your children. I don't believe it's too late to turn things around.

Hug the one you love – twice ☺

Lisa.

About the Author

Lisa Oliver had been writing non-fiction books for years when visions of half dressed, buff men started invading her dreams. Unable to resist the lure of her stories, Lisa decided to switch to fiction books, and now stories about her men clamor to get out from under her fingertips. With over fifty MM true mate titles to her credit so far, Lisa shows no sign of slowing down.

When Lisa is not writing, she is usually reading with a cup of tea always at hand. Her grown children and grandchildren sometimes try and pry her away from the computer and have found that the best way to do it is to promise her chocolate. Lisa will do anything for chocolate.

Lisa loves to hear from her readers and other writers (I really do, lol). You can catch up with her on any of the social media links below.

Facebook – http://www.facebook.com/lisaoliverauthor

Official Author page – https://www.facebook.com/LisaOliver ManloveAuthor/

My new private teaser group - https://www.facebook.com/groups/5 40361549650663/

And I am now on MeWe – you can find my group at http://mewe.com/join/lisa_olivers_pa ranormal_pack

My blog - (http://www.supernaturalsmut.com)

Twitter – http://www.twitter.com/wisecrone33 3

Email me directly at yoursintuitively@gmail.com.

Other Books By Lisa/Lee Oliver

Please note, I have now marked the books that contain mpreg and MMM for those of you who don't like to read those type of stories. Hope that helps ☺

Cloverleah Pack

Book 1 – The Reluctant Wolf – Kane and Shawn

Book 2 – The Runaway Cat – Griff and Diablo

Book 3 – When No Doesn't Cut It – Damien and Scott

Book 3.5 – Never Go Back – Scott and Damien's Trip and a free story about Malacai and Elijah

Book 4 – Calming the Enforcer – Troy and Anton

Book 5 – Getting Close to the Omega – Dean and Matthew

Book 6 – Fae for All – Jax, Aelfric and Fafnir (M/M/M)

Book 7 – Watching Out for Fangs – Josh and Vadim

Book 8 – Tangling with Bears – Tobias, Luke and Kurt (M/M/M)

Book 9 – Angel in Black Leather – Adair and Vassago

Book 9.5 – Scenes from Cloverleah – four short stories featuring the men we've come to love

Book 10 – On The Brink – Teilo, Raff and Nereus (M/M/M)

Book 11 – Don't Tempt Fate – Marius and Cathair

Book 12 – My Treasure to Keep – Thomas and Ivan

Book 13 – is on the list to be written – it will be about Wesley and yes, he will find his mate too, but that's all I can say about this one for now ☺ (Coming soon)

The Gods Made Me Do It (Cloverleah spin off series)

Book One - Get Over It – Madison and Sebastian's story

Book Two - You've Got to be Kidding – Poseidon and Claude (mpreg)

Book Three – Don't Fight It – Lasse and Jason

Book Four – Riding the Storm – Thor and Orin (mpreg elements [Jason from previous book gives birth in this one])

Book Five – I Can See You – Artemas and Silvanus (mpreg elements – Thor gives birth in this one)

Book Six – Someone to Hold Me – Hades and Ali (mpreg elements but no birth)

The Necromancer's Smile (This is a trilogy series under the name The Necromancer's Smile where the main couple, Dakar and Sy are the focus of all three books – these cannot be read as standalone).

Book One – Dakar and Sy – The Meeting

Book Two – Dakar and Sy – Family affairs

Book Three – Dakar and Sy – Taking Care of Business – (coming soon).

Bound and Bonded Series

Book One – Don't Touch – Levi and Steel

Book Two – Topping the Dom – Pearson and Dante

Book Three – Total Submission – Kyle and Teric

Book Four – Fighting Fangs – Ace and Devin

Book Five – No Mate of Mine – Roger and Cam

Book Six – Undesirable Mate – Phillip and Kellen

Stockton Wolves Series

Book One – Get off My Case – Shane and Dimitri

Book Two – Copping a Lot of Sin – Ben, Sin and Gabriel (M/M/M)

Book Three – Mace's Awakening – Mace and Roan

Book Four – Don't Bite – Trent and Alexi

Book Five – Tell Me the Truth – Captain Reynolds and Nico (mpreg)

Alpha and Omega Series

Book One – The Biker's Omega – Marly and Trent

Book Two – Dance Around the Cop – Zander and Terry

Book Three – Change of Plans - Q and Sully

Book Four – The Artist and His Alpha – Caden and Sean

Book Five – Harder in Heels – Ronan and Asaph

Book Six – A Touch of Spring – Bronson and Harley

Book Seven – If You Can't Stand The Heat – Wyatt and Stone (Previously published in an anthology)

Book Eight – Fagin's Folly – Fagin and Cooper

Book Nine – The Cub and His Alphas – Daniel, Zeke and Ty (MMM)

Book Ten – The One Thing Money Can't Buy – Cari and Quaid

Book Eleven – Precious Perfection – Devyn and Rex

Spin off from The Biker's Omega – BBQ, Bikes, and Bears – Clive and Roy

There will be more A&O books – This is my go-to series when I want to have fun.

Balance – Angels and Demons

The Viper's Heart – Raziel and Botis

Passion Punched King – Anael and Zagan

(Uriel and Haures's story will be coming soon)

Arrowtown

A Tiger's Tale – Ra and Seth (mpreg)

Snake Snack – Simon and Darwin (mpreg)

Liam's Lament – Liam Beau and Trent (MMM) (Mpreg)

Doc's Deputy – Deputy Joe and Doc (Mpreg)

NEW Series – City Dragons

Dragon's Heat – Dirk and Jon

Dragon's Fire – Samuel and Raoul

Dragon's Tears – (coming soon)

Standalone:

Bound by Blood – Max and Lyle – (a spin off from Cloverleah Pack #7)

The Power of the Bite – Dax and Zane

One Wrong Step – Robert and Syron

Uncaged – Carlin and Lucas (Shifter's Uprising in conjunction with Thomas Oliver)

Also under the penname Lee Oliver

Northern States Pack Series

Book One – Ranger's End Game – Ranger and Aiden

Book Two – Cam's Promise – Cam and Levi

Book Three – Under Sean's Protection – Sean and Kyle – (Coming soon)

Printed in Great Britain
by Amazon